Looking on the Heart
Life's Outtakes - Year 12

52 Humorous and Inspirational Short Stories

By
Daris Howard

A collection of stories, humorous anecdotes, thoughts, and tidbits of wisdom from the popular newspaper column.

Publishing Inspiration

Looking on the Heart

Life's Outtakes - Year 12

52 Humorous and Inspirational Short Stories

By

Daris W. Howard

A collection of stories, humorous anecdotes, thoughts, and tidbits of wisdom from the newspaper column *Life's Outtakes*.

Copyright © 2018
by
Daris W. Howard

ISBN-10: 1-62986-022-0
ISBN-13: 978-1-62986-022-0

www.publishinginspiration.com

Publishing Date:

Publishing Inspiration LLC

Table of Contents

Dear reader,

People often ask me if my stories are true. Though I must admit that I tend to take a bit of literary license in my writing, each story is based on an actual event. Sometimes the stranger stories are the ones that are stretched the least. As people often say, truth is stranger than fiction.

I also want to note that some of the names have been changed to protect the anonymity of the individuals.

Daris Howard

Friends and Paying It Forward

      We live in the region of the path of totality for the solar eclipse. Everyone in the area talked much of the year about ideas of how to use it to make money. We thought about it as well. We desperately need a new harp for our daughter since the one we have is starting to crack. A new harp is tens of thousands of dollars. We have a nice property with a pond, a pedal boat, canoes, and other fun things. We considered opening up our land for camping to earn money to put toward the harp.

      But as time went on, my feelings began to change. I didn't have a problem with having people on our land, but it was the concern I felt as I watched what was happening in our valley. Some hotels were raising the prices as high as ten times the normal rate. Many people who opened their land for parking and camping were also charging astronomical prices. A friend said he decided to rent the bedrooms in his house and wanted to be reasonable, but the price he charged was far beyond anything I could afford.

      As I started seeing lots of "Do Not Enter" signs and "No Trespassing" signs along the roads, I began to wonder how I would feel if I was someone from a long distance away who wanted to come see the eclipse and didn't have much money to spend. How welcome would I feel? I also thought of the times we had gone somewhere, and someone graciously invited us to camp on their property or shared what they had with us. I decided it was time to pay it forward.

      I talked to my family, and we all came to the agreement that this is what we wanted to do. We started posting out to our Facebook groups inviting people to come for free. We even invited people we didn't know to come if someone we knew and trusted recommended them. We also started trying to think of other ways we could make their stay nice without spending too much of our own money. I decided that for not too much, I could make Dutch oven potatoes and scones with honey butter the night before the eclipse, along with pancakes and eggs for breakfast the next morning.

All our available spots were filling quickly, mostly with people who could not afford to come if they had to pay rent. And though we were nervous, having never done anything like this before, we were growing more and more excited to see former friends and to meet new people. I started preparing the food early in the afternoon, and not long after the guests started arriving, it was ready. Everyone brought potluck dishes, and we added Dutch oven chicken. While I cooked, my wife and daughters helped or were friendly hostesses. We all had a wonderful time, and every guest felt to us like friends we had known all our lives.

We all visited until well after the stars had come out. There was only one bathroom, and as everyone was preparing for bed, the line was long, but all were patient.

The next morning, I was up early cooking pancakes, eggs, and hash browns. We had milk and water, and others shared juice, fruit, and cereal. There was plenty. Both children and adults canoed and swam in the pond, and our kittens were a major attraction.

As the time for the eclipse came, the kittens were put back into their home and were soon one big, sleepy pile. Everyone settled into chairs or lay on the lawn to watch. The excited squeal of the children when the eclipse reached totality brought excitement to everyone. And everyone laughed as our rooster started crowing, confused and thinking it was a new sunrise.

As everyone was packing up to head on their way, children wanted one more boat ride around the pond or one more chance to pet the kittens. Everyone hung around longer, enjoying the new friendships. But eventually, our home was quiet again, and when I finally sat down for the evening, I was exhausted but realized we had benefitted even more than those who had come to visit. Others I visited with who had done similar things said the same thing. I also learned something else that was very important: A person can never pay it forward without having even more come back to himself.

Bearly Keeping Up

I was joining the scouts of our community on a high adventure into the Jedediah Smith Wilderness, and it's bear country. It's not only bear country; it's grizzly country. That meant we needed to be prepared. All three of us men who were leaders were packing weapons, just in case. I was also carrying bear spray. I once had a dangerous encounter with a coyote pack that almost ended in disaster for me. I also had some close encounters with black bears and mountain lions, so I was taking no chances. None of us men expected to run into any trouble, and we definitely hoped we wouldn't, but we felt responsible for the young men in our charge and didn't want to take chances.

The boys, on the other hand, didn't seem to think twice about it. We had barely lifted the packs onto our backs for the five-mile hike into Hidden Lake before they were hiking fast and increasing the distance between themselves and us. They were young, healthy, and energetic, and we were much older, with declining energy. Our packs were also heavier since we were carrying extra items for the camp.

We pushed ourselves hard to make sure we stayed within calling distance of the boys, and by the time we arrived at the camp, I was exhausted. I was the oldest, and it seemed to wear on me the most. I set up my tent and just climbed into it, too tired to move for about an hour.

The boys, meanwhile, were off to fish at the lake. There were a lot more people around the lake, so we weren't too nervous about them being a little farther away, but we still tried to keep a watch in case there were any problems. We were careful to put our food into the somewhat broken-down bear box that was provided at the camp. And we made sure no one had any food in their tents so as not to attract bears. Though there were a few signs of bears, like claw marks on trees, none of them were fresh.

One boy claimed he heard a bear snorting in the middle of the night, but we finally determined that it was more likely somebody snoring. Still, we were cautious.

On the day we were to hike back out of the wilderness, the boys wanted to stay as long as they could. The fishing had been good, and they wanted to do some more before we left. This meant we wouldn't be hiking until the afternoon, and we would need to do a strong, fast hike to get out in time to get to our next campsite at Grassy Lake.

The boys came back from the lake later than expected. Though many of us had our gear packed to go, the ones who had been fishing still had to take down their tents and load them into their packs. So by the time we were ready to move out, the sun was starting down the western sky. This made the boys more anxious to hike faster.

The smallest boy also happened to be the scoutmaster's son. He weighed less than my pack, but he had more energy than an atomic explosion. He didn't want to be held back by us "old guys," wanting to hike at a much faster pace. Knowing this, his father warned him about the bears and told him to make sure he stayed close enough that he could hear and see us at all times so we could be there in an instant if there was a problem.

"Oh, Dad," he said, "I'll be fine. No bear could catch me."

"Jason," his father said, "a bear can outrun every human every time. And as small as you are, you would be nothing but a Scooby snack to a bear."

The second-smallest boy, Devon, decided to help out. Sounding grownup and talking as if he would be responsible, he said, "I'll keep up with Jason so he'll be okay."

As Jason's dad rolled his eyes, I laughed. "That will be great," I said. "Together, you two will just make a Scooby snack bonus pack."

Jason's dad laughed, but with that, we shouldered our packs and once more hiked fast to keep up, just in case the boys met a Scooby-snack-loving bear.

The Computer Mystery

Because I worked part-time for a government computer contractor doing internet development, the college where I worked decided to make use of those skills. My teaching was changed to part-time, with part of my assignment being the internet manager. I ran web servers, email servers, and some servers not commonly known today.

I had only been in my office for a short time one morning when my phone rang. On the other end of the line was the administrator of public relations, and he was irate. This was the first of many upset calls for the day.

"Professor Howard, the internet was down again this morning. That is the eighth time in the last two weeks."

"Yes," I replied. "The server is starting up now. It was off when I came into my office, and I started the boot process."

"This may not have been a problem before the internet was so critical to campus, or before email was so essential," the administrator said. "But now that so many people are getting used to using the internet for everything, we get lots of complaints when it's down. Is the computer having problems?"

"Not that I can tell," I answered. "When I pushed the button, it started right up. I have checked error logs and nothing indicates any computer error."

"Well, I want you to investigate and find out the problem," he said. "We can't have it happening anymore."

The college didn't feel that running the internet servers was even a part-time amount of work, so I was also the computer tech for four buildings. I was constantly called to deal with some issue. But I put every nonessential request on hold while I checked out every reason I could think of for the problem. But every idea I checked came to a dead end.

I called the physical facilities people to see if there were any power outages on campus. They said their systems didn't show any, so if there were any, they would have been only for an instant. We had battery backups on the computer that would have dealt with any short-term outage, and every indication from them was that they had never kicked on.

The system ran on Unix, and I turned on every logging system available. I went home that night, hoping that I would find the computer on the next morning, but it was off again, and I received more irate phone calls. The next night, I moved the server to the side and tried another one, but it was also off the next morning.

I started looking for patterns. I checked the other eight days. First, I found that the logs all showed that the computer went off at almost the same time each day, just after five o'clock a.m. All logs showed nothing beyond that early morning time, so it had to be an instant shutdown. I wondered if the CPU had overheated, and had shut down the system, but the CPU logs showed everything normal up to the instant that they went blank. Besides, it shouldn't have happened on both computers. With no idea what was causing the problem, I decided I would plan to be in my office by five o'clock so I could monitor the computer.

The next morning, I was up by four o'clock. I showered, ate breakfast, and was on my way. As I arrived at the office complex, I found a yellow cord trailing toward my office, and I could hear a vacuum. As I stepped through the door into my office, the lady from the cleaning crew was hard at work. I looked at the internet server, and to my dismay, it was already off. I had arrived too late.

The cleaning lady was a good friend, and when she saw me, she smiled and shut off the vacuum.

"Professor Howard," she said, "you need to be more careful. We are constantly reprimanded if we leave lights or other things on that waste electricity. And every morning, when I come in, I have found your computer running. But no need to worry, I have shut it off for you before anyone else could find out so you wouldn't get in trouble."

And thus, the computer mystery was solved.

Paying It Backward

My daughter Heather had a bad day. In fact, the whole week hadn't been that good. She had started school, and there was a mix-up in her classes. By the time she had that straightened out, a few days of class had already gone by. She then had to catch up, and there was the challenge of friends and everything else that goes with school starting.

She works at McDonald's, and, to top off her bad week, she had to work Friday and Saturday shifts. She worked the late shift Friday night until ten o'clock, and then she had to be back by six o'clock in the morning. By the time I picked her up from work on Friday, she was exhausted. She had purchased some food so she could eat on the way home and go right to bed. After she finished eating, she drowsed in the car the rest of the way.

After we pulled into our driveway, she sleepily made her way into the house and disappeared into her bedroom. She and I were both up by five o'clock Saturday morning so we could get some breakfast and get her to work on time. When I dropped her off at work, she was not in a good mood.

I went home and wrote homework papers for the doctoral degree on which I am working. I thought that I probably wasn't enjoying my day any more than she was enjoying hers.

When I picked her up at two o'clock in the afternoon, I wondered what kind of mood she would be in. I assumed she would just come out, plop into the car, and fall fast asleep. But to my surprise, she was totally animated.

"Dad," she said. "You won't believe what happened. The minute I clocked in, they assigned me to work at back-drive."

"What's back-drive?" I asked.

"That's the window that takes the money from people in the

8

drive-thru. Then the people pull their cars to front-drive, where they pick up their order."

"But I thought you hated drive-thru," I said.

"I always have before," she said. "But today was different. It started out bad. It was early in the morning, and it was almost always busy. And when it wasn't, I had to wash dishes. But then something happened. A car came through, and the man paid for his meal while his son continued searching for coins. After they paid, they didn't drive to the next window."

"Why not?" I asked.

"This is the fun part," she replied. "He asked me how much the order was for the car behind them. I told him, and then he paid that bill, and it was more than his own."

"Did he know the people in the next car?" I asked.

Heather shook her head. "I asked him, and he didn't."

"That was nice," I said.

"But here's something even more incredible," Heather said. "It didn't happen just once. It happened like a half-dozen times. And another thing that would happen was one person would pay for the next people, and then the next people would pay for the people behind them, and so on. The longest chain was seven cars in a row."

"Wow!" I replied

"The one that touched me the most," Heather said, "was the last chain. It had gone on for about five cars. Then, in the last car, there was a mother with five children. The children were hungry, and the littlest ones were crying. When they pulled up to pay, the tired mother was frantically searching through her purse. She finally turned to me and apologized because she didn't have the money. When I told her that the people in the car in front of her had already paid her bill, she started to cry, and she said she was so grateful."

Heather was quiet for a moment, and then she said, "There's nothing like seeing the goodness in people to make me feel happy."

Murder in the Dark

Donna and I had barely started dating. She played in the orchestra for a musical, so I went almost every night. One night after the musical finished, she invited me backstage. As we were mingling with other cast and orchestra members, one of them made an announcement.

"Hey, everyone, how would you all like to join us for a game of Murder in the Dark?"

"What's Murder in the Dark?" I asked Donna.

"Oh, it's a fun game," she answered. "I'm sure you'll love it. Come join us."

We went over to the black box theater. It was a room about twice the size of a normal classroom with bleachers on one side, and the rest was open floor space for the actors. Everyone took a seat on the bleachers while the actor who invited us gave the rules.

"Okay, for those who haven't played Murder in the Dark before, the rules are easy." He held up a bowl. "Papers are put into the bowl, one for each person. One paper will have a black dot. The person who gets it is the murderer. We then shut out the lights, and the murder wanders around the room. If he grabs someone, they are dead and have to sit on the bleachers. When the first person dies, he or she calls out one. As each successive person dies, they call out the next number. When half the people are dead, the game ends. Anyone who doesn't die is a survivor and scores a point."

"There's one other thing," a girl added. "The murderer has to hold onto you for three seconds. If you can get away within three seconds, you're not dead."

There were twenty-two people in the room. The papers were put into the bowl, and we each drew one. Then the lights were turned out. In the dark, occasionally, I would hear a scuffle, then a number would be called. Once eleven numbers were called, the lights came on.

I looked around the room. Donna was sitting on the bleachers. She had lost in that round. I hadn't felt the murder touch me at all. I had bumped into a few people, but each of them darted away from me as fast as I had from them.

Everyone drew a paper for round two. The lights went out, a few scuffles occurred, and a few numbers were called. Suddenly, I felt someone grab my shirt. I was on the varsity wrestling team, and we practiced hand control ad nauseam. Without even thinking, my reflexes kicked in. I grabbed the person's wrist and threw him across the room. I wasn't dead, but someone was groaning.

The person said, "I'm the murderer, but I think I was just killed. Turn on the lights."

The lights came on, and there on the floor, about twenty feet from me, was one of the actors. I thought I surely couldn't have tossed him that far, but I realized that adrenaline can do crazy things.

"So what happened?" somebody asked.

"I don't know," the murderer replied, as he slowly pulled himself to his feet. "All I know is I grabbed somebody, and in the next instant, I was flying across the room."

"Was it under three seconds?" a girl asked in a snickering tone.

"It was so fast, it must have been a half a second," he replied.

Everyone wanted to know who had gotten away. I was embarrassed and wanted to remain anonymous, but my shirt hung open with all the buttons ripped off, so I raised my hand.

One girl looked at where I stood compared to where the murderer was and gasped. "You threw him that far?"

I just shrugged. "Natural reflexes, I guess." They continued to stare at me, so I said, "How about I sit out this round and say I died?"

"You're okay with dying?" the girl asked.

"Sure," I replied. Then I called out, "Seven," as the lights went out, and I made my way to the bleachers.

I truly didn't mind. Donna was already out, so the bleachers were where I wanted to be anyway.

Looking on the Heart

Victor was in trouble again. It seemed that everywhere he went, he was in trouble. Part of the problem was he had been in six high schools in three years. It was hard for him to make friends. He would just start making some, and then his family would move again.

Victor had decided it wasn't worth trying. So, he grew his hair long, dressed like he was homeless, and walked around with an air of, "I don't care what anyone else thinks." When he would walk into the principal's office, or a counselor's office, or into any office, they immediately felt he was guilty because he looked guilty.

Now he was at a new school, and he was sure things wouldn't be any different. He had broken some rules and was sent to the principal's office. The principal grew exasperated with Victor's attitude and sent him to the counselor's office. When Victor knocked on the counseling office door, a man's voice called for him to come in. Victor sighed and opened the door. The man rose from his chair and came around the desk. The man extended his hand.

"I'm Rich. You must be Victor."

The kind tone of Rich's voice took Victor off guard. It was nonjudgmental. Victor slowly took the extended hand. Rich grasped Victor's hand tightly and shook it heartily.

"I'm glad you came to see me," Rich said. "I know you're new here, and I've been wanting to talk to you to see how it's going. It's nice of you to take the initiative on your own so I didn't have to find you."

Victor smiled. Rich made it sound like kindness on Victor's part that he was there. Victor knew that Rich had to have been informed why he came to the counseling office; otherwise, how would he know who Victor was when he walked in? Victor was especially amazed that Rich treated him like a best friend, not like a student who dressed rebelliously.

"So, how is it going?" Rich asked.

"All right, I suppose," Victor replied.

"You suppose?" Rich asked. "You don't know? When do you think you'll know?"

Rich laughed, and Victor laughed with him.

"I guess that did sound kind of funny, didn't it?" Victor said.

Victor felt comfortable, and he didn't feel judged for his appearance, so he found himself opening up and talking all about the moves and the lack of friends. He talked for quite a while, then ended with, "I guess I won't make any friends here, either."

"You know what I think?" Rich said. "I think from what you've told me, you're going about it backward."

"In what way?" Victor asked.

"It seems to me that you try to make friends, and then you try to like what they do. I think you need to decide what you like, do that, and make friends who enjoy the same activities. So, what do you like?"

Victor thought for a moment, then he said, "I like art. But most people think it's stupid."

"I don't," Rich said. "I admire anyone who can paint because I can't. And you're in luck, because we have an art club."

Rich got Victor involved in the art club, and soon, Victor had lots of friends. As the years went by, Victor's newfound friends became lifelong friends, and whenever Victor ran into Rich, Rich wanted to know how Victor's life was going. When Victor became a famous artist and had his work displayed in a national gallery, he came back especially to tell Rich.

"You didn't judge me when you saw me," Victor told him. "You believed in me. I'd like you to be my guest at the art exhibit."

"I'd love to," Rich said, "but there is one thing you should know. I'm blind."

Victor gasped. "Really?"

Rich nodded. "God took away my sight and replaced it with the blessing of being able to see the goodness of a person's heart instead."

Victor smiled, realizing that was exactly what Rich had done for him.

Mountain Climbing

I was scoutmaster to eighteen boys. They tried to challenge me at different times, and they had always come out the losers. Once, fourteen of them tried to throw me in a lake, and I got twelve of them in before the other two ran off. They didn't give up easily, though, and were determined to get me.

But then they learned I had a major weakness. I had promised the boys that I would do anything they wanted to do as long as it was safe and we stayed within the scout guidelines. One day, we hiked a high mountain, and they realized I was deathly afraid of heights. The mountain trail ran along a canyon wall. The other side of the trail was a steep drop to a river far below. I hugged the canyon wall, and the boys noticed.

"Daris, are you afraid of heights?" Gordy asked.

"Me," I said sarcastically. "Of course not. I'm just friends with the rocks on this wall."

The boys smiled at each other, and I knew they had something whirring around in their brains.

At the scout meeting the next week, as we planned for the following month, the boys grinned as Gordy made the announcement.

"We have decided we are going to work on the mountain climbing merit badge."

"It's getting awful late in the fall, don't you think?" I protested.

"You said you would do any scout thing we wanted to do," Mort said.

"But I also said it had to be safe," I complained.

My assistant scoutmaster could see what was going on, and he just grinned. He, too, had seen me on the hike and knew just what the boys were thinking. The more I tried to get out of it, the more determined the boys were to go.

At one scout camp in the mountains is a very tall climbing tower. It is far taller than any other climbing object in the area except for the mountains. This is what the boys wanted to climb, or I should say, this is what they wanted to see me climb. Mort said he'd see if he could schedule for us to go on a weekend. I secretly prayed it would be over-booked. But it wasn't, and the next weekend, we were all loading into my van and Rod's pickup to make the climb.

Once we arrived, we had to go through lots of instructions. Finally, it was time to climb. All of the boys and Rod climbed, then it was my turn. I was connected to a rope that went to the top of the tower and from there, down to Gordy, who was harnessed to a post. Shakily, I made my way slowly up the tower with the boys all cheering, or more appropriately, mocking me. Finally, I made it to the top. But the scout tower director would not let me climb on top.

"You've got to let go and trust your belayer, the person holding the rope, to let you down."

"Are you crazy?" I said. "I wouldn't trust him to fetch water right now."

"Well, then," he said, "you will have to hang there until you are too tired and have to let go."

I finally decided I couldn't hold on anymore, so I asked Gordy if he was ready. He said he was, so I let go.

Gordy was so confident in his ability to hold me that his harness was loosely buckled with some straps not connected at all. When I let go, my weight coming down jerked him out of the harness. He flew to the wall and slid up it as I slid down, both of us scraping on the plastic and wood blocks, passing each other in the middle.

When I finally hit the ground, I wasn't badly hurt, but my heart was pounding so hard I thought I'd have a heart attack.

"Hey, let me down," Gordy called as he dangled near the top of the tower.

"I ought to cut the rope and let you drop," I called back. "But at least that's over with."

"Au contraire," the tower director said. "For the merit badge, you have to do it three times."

That was one of the few times in life I really felt like maiming someone.

Keeping a Promise

My eighteen scouts were excited to see me do something I feared: earning the mountain climbing merit badge. But since I promised I would do any valid scout thing they wanted, I was stuck. My first climb up the tower was disastrous since the overconfident boy who was supposed to lower me back down didn't buckle in well. He was jerked out of the harness, and he passed me going up the tower as I came down. I thought I was done, but then I learned I had to make two more climbs.

Devin, who was more trustworthy, was my next belayer—the person holding the rope. I made sure he was buckled in tightly before I turned to make the ascent. I wasn't hurt in the first fall too much since Gordy's weight slowed my descent. But I still shook as I climbed so that I could hardly pull myself up. Finally, I reached the top.

"Devin, are you ready?" I called back over my shoulder.

"Sure," he said.

I took a deep breath and let go. Devin was tethered with a few feet of rope to a post. When I let go, my extra weight lifted him straight in the air. It scared him so badly that he let the rope slip, and I dropped about ten feet before the mechanism caught and stopped me. My heart was pounding, I was yelling, and the boys and Rod, the assistant scoutmaster, were laughing. That is, all of the boys except for Devin were laughing. He was dangling like a kite.

Rod and the other boys pulled Devin to the ground then held onto him until the rope could gradually be let out to get me down.

"Just one more climb, and you got it," the tower director said. "Which boy do you want on the rope for the last climb?"

"Boy, nothin'," I said. "A responsible adult is my belayer."

The tower director scowled. "You're supposed to trust your boys, but I suppose requirements say you just have to make the climbs."

Rod buckled in on the rope, and I started my last climb. By the time I got to the top, I was shaking so much I could hardly hold on.

"Are you ready, Rod?" I asked.

"Ready," he replied.

I wasn't sure I liked the chuckle in his voice, but I was too tired to hold on, so I let go. I immediately plunged down the side of the tower. I was in absolute freefall. I fell for over half the distance, and in that instant, I knew I was going to die. But suddenly, the rope pulled tight and stretched. Then I bounced upward about six feet and came down again. Like a spring, I went up and down, finally coming to a stop.

My heart was pounding so hard it had choked my voice to a gurgling gasping squeak. I couldn't even yell. When I finally came to a stop, and my head quit spinning, I did yell, but the boys and Rod were laughing so hard they could hardly hear me.

"What the devil kind of belaying was that?"

"Knowing how much you hate heights," Rod chortled, "I thought I'd get you down a little sooner by letting out a little extra rope at the beginning."

"Ha, ha," I yelled. "You think that's funny. Well, we'll just see how funny it is when I get down."

Rod laughed again. "You might want to be careful. I'm still the one deciding how much rope to let out."

By the time I got down, my chest felt like I had been lifting weights on the inside from the pounding of my heart.

Rod slapped me on the back. "You're a good sport. Let's all go get an ice-cream, and yours is on me."

"If I have my way," I replied, "It might just be on you."

By the time we got to town and purchased our ice-cream, I had cooled off. And as we ate, Mort said something that made it worth it.

"The main thing we'll always remember," he said, "is that you kept your promise, even when you were afraid."

How to Get the Girl

My wife, Donna, and I went to a restaurant. A couple came in, and we started visiting with them. We learned the husband's name was Brian, and his wife's name was Sarah. Donna asked them how they met.

Brian laughed. "When I went off to college, I struggled with getting dates. Finally, I asked my mother what I needed to do to find a girl who would marry me. She suggested I learn to play the piano and learn to dance. So, the next semester, the first thing I did was sign up for a piano class. The next thing I did was sign up for a dance class. I thought I had it made because both were full of girls. In fact, I was the only boy in the piano class."

"Maybe your mother was on to something," I said.

Brian nodded. "One of the things I quickly learned was that many of the girls were in those classes hoping to find a guy. I thought it was perfect."

"So, that's how you met?" I asked.

"In a sense," Brian replied. "I was so bad at dancing that after a while, the girls were reluctant to dance with me and didn't want anything to do with me."

"What about piano class?" Donna asked.

"It wasn't any better," Brian replied. "I found that I was almost tone-deaf. I couldn't even tell when I had made a mistake. After one turn of playing for the class, the girls suggested that maybe I could just play for the teacher's aide instead. They didn't want to listen to me. I also realized that is part of the reason I was a bad dancer. I also couldn't sense rhythm."

Donna turned to Sarah. "So, how do you fit into the story?"

"Well," Sarah said, "I was the teacher's aide for the piano class. The students had to play for me at different intervals during the semester so I could grade them on their improvement. In the midst of all the girls, there was one good-looking guy. I was excited when he walked in. But then he played the piano, and he was so bad, I was immediately annoyed with him. And to top it off, the teacher requested that Brian play for me what he should have played for the class."

"I was so bad Sarah thought I must not be practicing at all," Brian added.

"He claimed he did," Sarah said, "but I doubted it. In fact, I decided to listen outside his practice room. Sure enough, he practiced, but he'd miss a note and not even realize it was wrong. He was not getting any better because he didn't know enough to correct his mistakes. I just couldn't stand it, so I started going into the practice room with him, and I would reach around him and hit the right note when he missed one."

"At first, I was only playing with one hand," Brian said. "But eventually, we got to two hands, and sometimes I made a mistake on both hands at the same time. Then she would reach around me with both hands and hit the right notes."

"It was enough to grate on a person," Sarah said. "I couldn't stand it and just had to fix it."

Brian grinned. "But then I got thinking: I have a girl putting her arms around me. What could be better? I can't say that I made the mistakes on purpose because I didn't even know if I did it wrong in the first place. But I didn't really care if I hit the right notes or not if she was going to put her arms around me."

"Eventually, his smile and humor won out over his bad music," Sarah said. "I fell for him and enjoyed putting my arms around him. But when he asked me to marry him, I agreed on one condition. Unless a miracle occurred, and he somehow figured out how to play the piano, he was to never play it when I was around."

Brian laughed. "And I was happy to do that because I already had what I took piano for anyway!"

A Halloween Cat Attack

Lenny and his uncle always tried to get the best of each other on Halloween. Most of the time, Lenny's uncle won, but Lenny never gave up. This year, he decided he had a perfect plan.

The way he came up with the idea was purely by accident. He decided to take a shortcut through Old Mrs. Beaton's yard. Mrs. Beaton always played the part of the fragile widow woman, but anyone who had ever been chased by her swinging her broom knew better. And to add to that, she had an old black cat that Lenny was sure was possessed with something, perhaps it was the same stuff Mrs. Beaton drank.

Whatever it was, on the night Lenny cut through the yard, the cat was waiting for him. It had climbed the gatepost, and when Lenny went through in the dark, the cat launched out at him like a panther coming out of a jungle canopy. Lenny barely knew what hit him as he was knocked to the ground with the hissing, snarling little beast on him. He was still trying to fend it off and make a break for it when Mrs. Beaton came flying out of her house, swinging her broom like a cavewoman taking down a mammoth.

That was motivation for Lenny, and he ran nearly a quarter mile down the road with the little black hitchhiker still clawed onto his back. But what annoyed Lenny the most was if anyone ever mentioned how mean her cat was, Mrs. Beaton always said, "O poppycock. Phantom is as gentle as a lamb."

So, it was after the latest run-in with Phantom, whom Lenny called "Devil Cat," that Lenny got the idea of how he could get his uncle and the cat, too. Of course, no Halloween prank would be complete without enlisting Butch and Buster, his two neighbor friends.

"You want us to help you do what?" Buster said.

"I need you to help me catch Devil Cat," Lenny said.

"Are you crazy?" Butch said. "That cat thinks it's a lion and we're gazelles."

Lenny nodded. "I know. That's why it will be that much more fun."

With a little bribery, Butch and Buster agreed to help. On Halloween morning, they snuck behind Mrs. Beaton's barn. Lenny was carrying his dad's raccoon trap, and Buster was carrying meat.

"Butch," Lenny said, "go where Devil Cat can see you, but don't let Mrs. Beaton catch you."

"Why me?" Butch complained.

"Because you're not doing anything else."

Butch grudgingly went to act as the trespasser and soon came running back with Phantom close behind. Lenny and Buster had barely gotten the trap set and baited. All three ran until Phantom quit chasing them. When Phantom headed home, the boys followed at a distance.

The trap worked just like Lenny had hoped. Phantom smelled the meat and was soon locked inside. Lenny carried the trapped cat with Butch and Buster following. They circled wide around Mrs. Beaton's house. Lenny was glad that she had a long road back into her house so she wouldn't see them at her mailbox. They snuck up to the mailbox and released the snarling cat into it. The mailbox had vents so the cat would be fine, but it hissed and fumed. Finally, in the dim light inside the mailbox, it went silent.

It was none too soon. The boys had barely hidden when Lenny's uncle, the new mail-delivery person, came driving into view. The boys waited in the willows and watched. Finally came the moment Lenny had dreamed of. With the car window down, Lenny's uncle opened the little mailbox door to stick in the mail.

The cat, seeing a chance to escape, jumped into the car. Finding itself caged, it flew around the car, ripping everything it could get its claws on. Lenny's uncle panicked, let off the brake, then hit it, then let off. The car lurched in zigzags across the road as Lenny's uncle tried to fight off the cat and get away from it. Finally, the cat, seeing the open window, left Lenny's uncle a few tattoos of her affection for him and jumped to her freedom.

The next Sunday at church, Lenny's uncle was still sporting some bandages.

"Hey, Uncle, what happened to you?" Lenny asked with a smirk.

"A no-good nephew is what happened," he replied. "But just you wait! Halloween will come around again next year."

The Snow Game

As we finished up football practice before our last season game, our coach pulled us all together.

"I checked the weather report, and it predicts blowing snow tomorrow, so dress warm."

The next morning when I milked the cows, it was freezing, and the wind was blowing. I had already played a game on a frozen field of ice and didn't relish the thought of experiencing that again.

As we gathered after school as a football team, Coach called a meeting.

"With the temperature where it is, no one would blame us if we canceled the game. But if we do, it would count as a forfeit to the other team. What do you want to do?"

The snow had just started falling, and the wind was whipping it everywhere. Despite this, we unanimously voted to play.

We made the trip to the other school, which was quite a distance away, a trip made longer on icy roads. We found out that the other team thought we would cancel and weren't ready to play. No thought had been given to clearing the field, and it was still a foot deep in snow. A snowblower was run down both sides of the field so we could see the sidelines. Though it was still snowing, the clouds had partially cleared, and the temperature had dropped further. It was close to zero. The wind was blowing ice crystals of snow that felt like miniature needles into exposed skin.

The other team, being a home team, set up lots of gas heaters for themselves. Two fathers from our team had each brought one. We got one, and the cheerleaders got the other. But I didn't have to worry. I was first-team offensive line, first-team defensive line, and the kicker.

I was always on the field and kept moving and stayed warm. It was the guys who were in and would get sweaty then would go out and freeze that I felt sorry for. They would huddle around the heater trying to stay warm.

Our cheerleaders were dressed in big parkas. They would break apart to do a quick cheer if we made a big play, then they would huddle around their heater.

"We don't have cheerleaders," Lenny said. "We have supporting polar bears."

Even the refs had their striped shirts over big, thick coats and looked like over-stuffed zebras.

We won the toss, so I got to do the first kick of the game. When I kicked, I got it off well, but my other foot slipped, and I went down flat on my back. The other team receiver slipped, couldn't get the ball, and it bounced into the end zone. They fumbled the next play, but as we flopped around in the snow, it was hard to tell where the ball was.

The game went much the same way. The wind whipped snow into our faces, making it hard to tell who was where and especially where the ball was. At one point, their quarterback dropped back to pass. I busted through the line and headed for him. He backpedaled and threw it at the last minute. I couldn't stop and plowed through him and the ref behind him. The quarterback wanted a late hit called, but the ref pointed to my skid mark as evidence that I tried to stop.

When halftime came, we were down twenty-eight to seven. We gathered in the locker room for the half-time pep talk.

"Howard," Coach said, "you have had more than half the tackles and most of the blocks. Why are you doing so well compared to everyone else?"

"I'm always on the field and stay warm," I replied.

Coach thought about that and said, "We receive this half. If, as offense, you can make a touchdown, we'll just do onside kicks to try to keep you out there so you can stay warm."

When we came out, the cheerleaders wished us good luck and went home. So did most of the crowd. Only about a dozen spectators stayed to support each team.

We received the ball and marched down the field for a touchdown. We kicked onside, and in the powdery free-for-all, we got it. We continued this, and our offense was never off of the field, except for the kicks, and we won forty-one to thirty-five.

As we left the field and headed for the bus, Lenny said, "Howard, remind me what sport that was we were playing, because it sure wasn't football."

The Touch Lamp

My daughter, Heather, came out of her room all bleary-eyed one morning.

"What happened to you?" I asked.

"My touch lamp is broken," she said. "At least, I hope that's all it is."

"How would that make you so tired?"

"It freaked me out all night," she replied. "It would turn on by itself. I would reach over and turn it off, and then a while later, it would turn on again. I finally decided I didn't care, so I just left it on, but then it would turn itself off. I tried to ignore it, but the turning on and off about every half hour or so was kind of spooky."

"I'm surprised it has gone bad so fast," I said. "It's practically new."

She shrugged, half asleep. "Whatever. All I know is it kept me awake most of the night. And if it's not the lamp's fault, I'm not sure I want to know what it is."

I consider myself a fairly decent electrician, so I took the lamp apart to look at it. I couldn't find any short or anything that seemed wrong. I took it down and set it in the living room by my chair. Anytime I was near it, I would touch it. If it was on, it turned off, and if it was off, it turned on. It never seemed to do anything on its own. I figured it was just a fluke.

We put the lamp back in Heather's room, but the next morning, she complained about the same thing happening. I decided to try it in my room. I turned it off for the night, and never once did it turn on by itself.

We tried it in her room again, but the next morning, she was sleeping on the couch and complained about the same thing happening.

I read everything I could find about touch lamps and could find nothing that indicated the kind of problem we were having. I hated to get rid of it since it was so new, but I didn't know what else to do.

Then one night, Heather was going to be late after getting home from a school activity, so I had her set up her room just like she would for bed. While she was gone, I watched her room. I made sure the light was off, and when I came back later, it was on. I shut it off, and when I came back later, it was on. I left it on and came back later, and it was off. It was spooky.

I decided I was going to get to the bottom of it, so I went in and sat on her bed. As I sat there, I heard the familiar buzzing sound that is so annoying when a person is trying to sleep. It was the sound of a fly. It sounded like a really big one. I considered getting up and getting a fly swatter when I thought of something else.

I realized it was attracted to the night light by Heather's bed. That night light was right next to her lamp. I wondered if the answer could be what I was thinking. I waited, and momentarily, the light turned on. I looked at the lamp, and the fly was sitting on it. I continued to watch the fly. Eventually, it flew away. I could hear it buzzing around. It landed somewhere. I continued to listen, and it started buzzing again. Eventually, I could see it coming back, and it landed on the lamp. The lamp instantly shut off.

I got up off of the bed and turned on the main light. I chased the fly from the room with a fly swatter and moved the night light over by the desk, so if there were ever a fly again, it would be attracted in that direction. That night, when Heather came home, I told her I had found her ghost.

When I told her what it was, she looked at me suspiciously, but the ghost never came back, and the lamp was saved from a trip to the second-hand store.

Comforting a Child

We were in New York one summer, a long way from our home in Idaho, when it happened. Our little four-year-old daughter, Elliana, broke her arm on a trampoline. Doctors often say that trampolines are one of the most dangerous inventions ever made, at least for children. But in this case, she was only sitting on the edge of it eating ice cream when someone walked across it, and she fell off.

We hoped it was only a sprain, but when we looked at it, we knew it was broken. We took her to a local medical clinic, but they said it was bad enough that she had to go to the main hospital in the middle of the city. They gave her some pain medicine and sent us on our way. I had lived and worked in that city in my younger years, and I knew that the hospital was in a rough part of town. I was not anxious to take my daughter there, but I didn't have much choice.

My wife and I left the rest of our children with a friend, and we took Elliana to the hospital. When we arrived at the emergency room, it was full of people. The nurse told us that some of them were just homeless and didn't know where else to go, so the security would eventually help them find shelter. However, she also told us that many of the others were in for drug overdoses and such things and would have to be seen at a higher priority than Elliana since her injury, though painful, was not life-threatening.

To try to comfort her, I told her that when we got done, we would buy her a nice treat. She lay in my arms and whimpered from the pain, but she never complained. I tried to make her as comfortable as I could, but as any parent would be, I was concerned for her. The hours went by, and finally, after what seemed like forever, it was our turn. We were taken to a small room. Eventually, a doctor came to see her. He checked her arm and said he would need some x-rays of it. I asked if I should carry her down to the x-ray room.

He shook his head. "We will have to have a member of the union responsible for transporting patients do that."

We sat in the room for another half hour before a man showed up and told us he was there to take her to the x-ray room, which ended up being only about twenty feet down the hall. Once we were inside, the man left. The x-ray technician started to move the camera into place, and this scared Elliana. I comforted her by telling her it was just a big camera, and he was going to take some pictures of her.

"Be good and let him do it, and remember that when we get all done, we'll get you a fun treat," I said.

My wife and I had to be in the control room away from the x-rays, and I was afraid Elliana would be frightened when we stepped out. But she stayed calm and held still for the x-rays. After they were taken, I lifted her into my arms again, and we were forced to sit and wait another half hour for the man to come back to take her twenty feet back to the other room again.

After another short time, the doctor and a nurse came in. They worked together to set Elliana's arm and put on a cast. Through it all, Elliana was really good.

Finally, it was all over, and we were able to leave. We went back to pick up the other children before going, as promised, to get Elliana a special treat. The other children all gathered around to look at the cast.

"How was it?" Elliana's sister asked her.

"It wasn't much fun," she replied. "But Daddy promised me a treat when we got done. So, I tried to be really good, even when the man used the scary camera."

"It was an x-ray machine," I explained.

"And," Elliana said, "even though my arm hurt, I was especially good for the camera. I smiled for every picture."

And I smiled as we loaded in the van to buy her the biggest candy bar we could find in the store.

Thanksgiving and Freedom

The year was 1941. There was news of the carnage in Europe and Asia, and many were grateful America was not involved. The country faced the hardship of the Great Depression, and even though Arden's little community wasn't spared, everyone had shared food and other necessities. Though there were shortages, everyone had plenty to eat and a place to live.

Arden was a leader in the community, and he felt the need for a special Thanksgiving Day dinner. He and other community leaders organized it, but they wondered who the speaker should be. Someone suggested Ben. He was the scoutmaster and had been for many years. His love for the country and his gratitude for life was evident in how he lived and how he trained the boys.

Everyone agreed that Ben was the perfect choice. When asked, Ben gladly accepted. He asked if his scouts could post the colors. Everyone thought that would be a good idea.

Almost everyone in the community came to the dinner. Though money was scarce, the harvest had been good and food was plentiful. Ben came smartly dressed in his scoutmaster uniform. The boys were all in their uniforms, too. The flag ceremony was impressive. Ben had taught the boys well.

Ben's talk was a great tribute to the country. He told of his great-grandparents immigrating to the United States and how life was hard, but they loved this country. They passed that love to their children. Ben said that after he was born, that same love of country was passed on to him. He was proud to wear the scout uniform that had the American flag emblem on it. He talked about community and togetherness and the great goodness and friendship he felt there.

After his talk, a blessing was given, and everyone joined in for a wonderful dinner. The food was outstanding, and the friendship and the love of country was felt by all.

Then, only a few weeks later, the Japanese bombed Pearl Harbor. With that act, the United States entered the war. But what bothered Arden most was the divisiveness that act had sown in his community. Many people demanded a meeting, and when Arden heard what it was to be about, it saddened him. But there was little he could do except hold the requested meeting.

The meeting had barely been called to order when Mr. Weber rose to address the group. "As you all know, we are now at war with Japan. I am concerned about having a Japanese man as scoutmaster to our boys."

"I agree," Mr. Lombardi said. "He could be a spy."

"But Ben has been one of the best scoutmasters this community has ever known," Mr. Anderson said. "I trust him completely with my sons."

This discussion went back and forth for quite a while. Most were against Ben and anyone who looked like him. Arden was sickened that this community that had pulled together through the tough years of the depression was willing to turn on the few whom they now looked on with distrust because of their skin color. What had happened to that spirit of friendship that had been at the Thanksgiving dinner only a few weeks earlier? Then he thought of something else.

Arden arose to speak. "It is true that we are at war with Japan. But are we not also at war with Germany and Italy?"

"What has that to do with it?" Mr. Weber asked.

"Isn't Weber a German name?" Arden asked. "And how about Lombardi? Isn't that Italian?" Suddenly, the room went quiet as Arden continued. "Ben's family has been here for many generations, longer than some of ours. And I know my heritage is from many countries, including Germany. But I am a US citizen, not a German citizen, and Ben is a US citizen, too. If any person in this room claims no heritage foreign to this country, let him stand."

With that, David Brown-Bear, an Indian, stood. Everyone, including Arden, laughed.

David Brown Bear said, "I stand in support of Ben, as I have often been considered an outsider in my own land."

The message was well understood, and no one else spoke. The meeting quickly adjourned, and everyone slipped off into the night.

A couple of months later, as Ben left on the train to fight for his country, the whole community was there to proudly shake his hand.

The Friendly Cow

When the economy started going down in 2008, my wife, Donna, thought we ought to consider getting a milk cow. We called around and found a Jersey dairy and asked if they might sell us one.

"I'm sure we could find something," Dallin, the owner, said.

Donna and I drove to the dairy, pulling our horse trailer behind our van. When we got there, Dallin said he had three cows from which we could choose. I knew that a dairy farm never sells their best cows, so I asked what was wrong with them.

Dallin pointed at the first one. "This cow is a little bit wild."

I decided that one was out. If I ever had to be gone, and my children needed to milk the cow, I wanted her to be gentle.

Dallin pointed at the second cow. "This cow only has three good teats."

I considered this cow for a moment. I was going to be milking by hand but eventually hoped to get a milker. Keeping a milker on a cow with three teats was hard.

We went to the pasture to look at the last cow. She was a solid-looking cow, with good form, and I knew she was probably a decent milker. I figured she must have a bad disposition.

"This cow is . . ." Dallin paused and thought a minute before he continued. "I'm not quite sure how to describe her."

"Is she mean?" I asked.

"Quite the contrary," he replied. "She's too friendly. The problem is, my children raised her as a pet, and she feels she's part of the family. She's bossy and tells the other cows what to do. I think that's because she feels that as a family member, she's superior to them. She also likes to be petted, and I mean she likes it a lot."

It was at this point that the cow saw us, and she headed quickly in our direction. She came up and pushed her head right into my stomach quite forcefully.

"She's asking you to pet her," Dallin said.

I thought, "She isn't asking, she's telling."

"She might work well as a single cow," Dallin said. "With no other cows to boss around, she should get along okay."

She did seem to be the best cow of the three, so I decided she would be the one. As we walked back to the yard where the horse trailer was parked, the cow followed us, staying right next to me so I could pet her. I had to watch my feet so she wouldn't step on them.

"Will she load okay into our horse trailer?" I asked.

Dallin shrugged. "Never tried. But my guess is, knowing her, if you were to go in first, taking some grain with you and petting her, you could coax her right in. Do you have a front door on the trailer you can go out?"

"Yes," I replied. "It's a small one, but I think I can squeeze through it."

And that's exactly what I did. I backed into the trailer, holding out the bucket and scratching the cow's head. She followed me in, with her head buried in the bucket eating the grain. Once I had her in, Dallin shut the back door, and I climbed out the front one.

"Just don't forget to scratch her ears when you turn her out of the barn," Dallin said. "She doesn't like it if you forget."

I said I would remember, paid him the money, and we were on our way.

For a while, I remembered what Dallin said, but one day I forgot. I milked her and turned her out of the stall, then started spreading straw in the barn. The cow stood patiently for about ten seconds, then she pushed her head into my back, shoving me against the wall. For about ten minutes, I tried to whack her to get her to let me go, but nothing worked. Finally, I remembered what Dallin said. I was able to reach one hand around enough to scratch behind one ear.

She let me go and turned the other ear for me to scratch it. Once I had finished, she went off to her pasture.

And that's when I realized why Dallin decided to sell a "too friendly" cow.

A Friendly Cow, Again

Justin, a young man who was a friend with our daughter, learned that we had a pond stocked with fish. In the fall, the water is cut out of the canal that feeds the pond, so we have to catch all the fish out of it. Justin asked if he could come help with that task. I told my daughter it would be fine, but he needed to call before he came.

Justin had grown up in a city and knew nothing about farm animals. He had recently moved to our area. He'd never been fishing until he moved here, but the first time he did, he was hooked. He spent every minute he could at it, often heading out right after school each evening.

One evening, when I arrived home, my wife informed me that Justin was coming.

"When?" I asked.

She shrugged. "This evening. For all I know, he could already be here."

"Oh, no," I said. "I better get out there. I let Leah graze by the pond today."

When we bought our cow, Leah, the owner took me out to pick from three cows he was selling. One was mean, one only had three teats, and the third seemed perfect. He said her only problem was she was too friendly. I couldn't understand how a cow could be too friendly, so I bought her. But I learned what he meant the first time she shoved me up against the barn wall because I forgot to pet her. Leah was a friendly cow, alright. But she didn't just ask for attention, she demanded it. She especially liked her ears scratched.

I considered changing my clothes before heading out to the pond but decided that just in case Justin was already there, I'd better not. I rushed outside and looked toward the pond. Sure enough, I could see Justin's car. As I neared the pond, I could hear screaming, so

38

I quickened my pace. As I grew nearer, I could see Justin at a full run with Leah right behind him.

Our pond is about forty yards in circumference, and they were running around it. They were coming at a fast clip and passed as I was approaching. I yelled for Justin to stop and scratch her ears. He either didn't hear me, or in his panicked state, he didn't trust what I was saying.

They did another lap and passed me again before I could get through the fence. I ran after them, yelling for Justin to stop, but he didn't. However, either my yelling distracted him, or he was growing tired, but either way, he slowed, and Leah cut him off and cornered him against the fence.

I ran toward them as Leah stepped closer and closer. Justin had his head turned from her and was trembling with fear, his eyes closed. Just before I reached them, Leah reached out her tongue and licked the side of Justin's face.

If you haven't been licked by a cow and would like to know what it feels like, consider running as fast as you can toward a gravel road and jumping face-first into it. That would be a similar sensation. A cow's tongue is about as coarse as forty-grit sandpaper, the roughest kind.

When Leah licked Justin's face, he screamed like he was being killed. It was about this time that I reached them. I started to scratch behind Leah's ears, and she turned her attention to me. She leaned her head toward me so I could scratch the other ear. Justin still had his eyes closed, but finally, he opened them a little. When he saw me, he let out a big exhale of air as if he had been holding his breath.

He gasped, "Your bull . . . your bull was trying to kill me."

"First off," I said, "she's a cow, not a bull. And secondly, she only wanted her ears scratched."

I had him scratch Leah's ears, and he did so with a trembling hand. Then I locked her in her pasture, because it's hard to scratch a cow's ears and fish at the same time.

The Friendly Cow Returns

Our cow, Leah, demanded to be petted. Justin, our daughter's friend, learned that when he came out to fish in our pond. Leah chased him until she had him cornered. I arrived just in time to pet her and save him. I explained to him that Leah was just being friendly and wanted him to scratch her ears.

"What would she do if a person didn't scratch her ears?" Justin asked.

"When I didn't, she shoved her head in my back and pushed until she had me pinned against the barn wall," I replied.

I locked Leah in a pasture away from the pond so Justin could fish in peace.

A couple of days later, Justin called and asked if he could bring a roommate and go fishing again.

"Sure," I replied. "Just let me know ahead of time so I can lock Leah out of the pond area."

"It's okay," he said. "Now that I know what she will do and that she isn't going to kill us, I will be fine."

Justin and his roommate did come fishing. I wasn't home when they came, nor did I worry about them. I had shown Justin how to lead her into the pasture and how to secure the gate. I figured that Justin could take care of things if he needed to.

A few days after he came fishing, my daughter informed me that there was a video she had on her phone that I needed to watch.

"What is it?" I asked.

"It's Justin and his roommate fishing," she replied.

"Did they pull out some big ones?"

She laughed and said, "You'll just have to watch it. Justin didn't tell his roommate everything about Leah. He just said if she came up close, it didn't matter because she was friendly and wouldn't hurt anyone."

My daughter turned on the video, and we watched it.

The roommate climbed through the fence in by the pond. He walked over to the fishing area. Leah, seeing someone whom she thought had a duty to pet her, immediately came over. Justin had told his roommate not to run or Leah would give chase. That was the mistake Justin made when he first came. But the roommate didn't run. He just started fishing.

He didn't run, but he also didn't scratch Leah's ears, so she moved in closer. As he kept fishing, she kept moving closer, but he didn't take the hint. Finally, she had her head right against his back. But the roommate didn't know she expected him to pet her, so he tried to push her away with one hand while he held the fishing pole with the other.

Leah must have decided it was time to show this stranger she meant business, so she bunted him with her head, sending him flying into the pond. At this point, the camera jiggles a lot and moves closer as Justin is apparently laughing and walking to the pond. But after a moment of the camera recording the roommate trying to pull himself from the water, the camera suddenly goes upward, and all a person can see is the sky. Then, after a brief moment, the video ends.

"What happened at the end?" I asked.

My daughter laughed. "Justin had planned all of this, thinking Leah might push his roommate into the pond. But the one thing he didn't remember in his calculations was that Leah was still there. After he came up to laugh at his roommate and film him in the water, Leah decided Justin should pet her. But he was too busy to pet her, so she shoved him in the pond, too. Luckily he was able to hold his phone up out of the water."

At least Leah was equal in her ear-scratching expectations.

Competition for Good

It had been a hard year in our rural community. Lots of older people had passed away, leaving their spouses alone. There had also been quite a few farm accidents from which people were recovering. To add to that, farm prices were low, and many in our community were looking toward the upcoming year knowing it would be hard to make ends meet.

With Christmas coming, the men and women decided to have a friendly competition. It was all in the sake of doing good and lifting the hearts of friends and neighbors who needed to know that someone cared about them. The women challenged the men to see who could do the most good deeds. The loser would be responsible for the community Christmas dinner.

The competition would be based on the number of events that were done and the total number of hours put into the projects. If each group won one, it would be considered a tie.

Samuel, the community leader, called a meeting of the men to discuss different projects that were needed. He started the meeting and opened the floor for discussion.

"One of the first things we need to do is to make sure everyone has a good supply of wood for winter," Ben said.

Everyone agreed that this was the highest priority. Samuel asked if anyone knew where we could get wood.

"There are lots of old trees along the fence that runs through my pasture," Harold said. "I would love to have them cut down and cleaned up."

A time was set for the wood project, then other ideas were suggested. These included shoveling snow, since the forecast said it was imminent. The young men said they'd clean yards for the elderly.

Projects were lined up through November and most of the way to Christmas.

Through that time, we worked hard. I chopped wood, shoveled snow, and raked and cleaned. Almost every weekend and many evenings, I joined with the men or the boys doing some service work. While we were doing our part, the women were baking food and taking it to people to cheer their hearts. Families who had more shared with families who had less. This work did as much for those who provided it as for those who were the beneficiaries. By Christmas, the glow of the spirit of the season could be felt in every home.

Just before the day of the community dinner, everyone recorded their hours as best they could remember. Everyone had gotten so caught up in the spirit of sharing and giving that the contest was almost forgotten. But in a fun way, everyone wanted to see who was going to be responsible for organizing the dinner.

After the hours and work were all submitted, they were tallied, and both the men and the women met together. I was sitting up front near Samuel, and he asked me to start the meeting while he looked over the report. After I had given the preliminaries and reminded everyone about the community Christmas dinner, I turned the time over to Samuel.

Samuel stepped to the microphone to address us. "Men," he said, "I have looked things over, and the women have much better figures than we have."

His phraseology caught me by surprise, and I started laughing. Samuel turned to glare at me, and I covered my mouth to try to hold back my mirth. No one else seemed to find it funny.

John, the old man next to me, chided me. "Daris, it's rude to laugh when Samuel is speaking."

I repeated Samuel's words to John, and his eyes lit up with the understanding of what I found so funny. He, too, started to laugh. "That's rich," he said. "Like it really takes much looking things over to see that the women have better figures than we have." Then he laughed harder.

Samuel turned to glare at John and me. And since no one else laughed, John and I were assigned to be in charge of the Christmas dinner. But the women all helped because, besides having better figures, they were also better cooks.

Together Forever

Being a foster parent can be both a heartwarming and heartbreaking experience. That was the case with a nine-year-old boy who lived with us for whom I will use the name Charlie to protect his identity. Charlie and his two sisters were taken into foster care because of the harsh conditions in their home. Charlie had also endured a lot of abuse from his father.

One day, my wife, Donna, was driving the van with Charlie in it, along with our own children. Suddenly, Charlie began to scream, scaring everyone.

"That's his house! He'll get me!"

Donna was panicked by the sudden outburst, and Charlie was shaking uncontrollably. Donna had Charlie lie down on the seat so whoever he feared wouldn't see him.

"Who will get you?" she asked.

"My father will!" Charlie said. "That's his house we just passed!"

Donna promised Charlie she would protect him, and Charlie calmed down. That night, Charlie showed us his scars where his father had burned him with a lit cigarette.

One heartwarming part of the experience with Charlie was seeing the love he had for his two younger sisters. They were in another foster home about two hours away. He asked to call them every day. When September came, with our eight children plus one extra, we started planning and working toward Christmas. When we asked Charlie what he wanted for Christmas, his answer didn't surprise us.

"I want to be with my sisters and never be separated from them again."

I felt empathy for this little boy and wished we could have his sisters in our home, but it was out of our hands. And not long after we had this conversation, childcare services called and said they were moving Charlie to another home. When a judge had asked Charlie's mother how often she came to visit him, she said it was too far away, so she hadn't. We lived about half an hour from her and were willing to take Charlie to visit her, but she always said she was too busy. Despite this, the judge ordered Charlie to be moved to a home closer to her.

A home was located with a family who didn't really want him, and it was hard to have him taken from us. One other sad part of being a foster parent is that once a child is moved from your home, you seldom hear how they are doing.

On the morning of December 26th of that year, as my family still slept, I sat down to read the paper. The headline said three children had died in a fire. I gasped when I saw Charlie's name among them. As the story unfolded over the next couple of weeks, we learned that he and his sisters had been put back into the home with their mother and her boyfriend. During the week before Christmas, Charlie had shoveled every walk in the neighborhood to earn money to buy his sisters Christmas presents, the only ones they had.

All the neighbors loved the three children and were happy to help Charlie with his endeavors. But the mobile home they lived in was not clean, and on Christmas night, one of the heaters in the mobile home caught some clothes on fire, which in turn caught the home on fire. As the home burned, the children's mother calmly walked to the neighbors to tell them the house was on fire while her boyfriend saved his car. The neighbors rushed to pull the children from the fire, but the children died of smoke inhalation.

Some in the community felt the mother and her boyfriend must have been high on something, as calm as they were, and wanted charges filed. But the mother and her boyfriend quickly left the area. We never told our children anything about Charlie until many years later.

As I struggled with my grief for the loss of this little boy we had grown to love, the memory of his Christmas wish came back to me. As hard as it was to know he was gone, I wondered if God had granted Charlie's wish, and on Christmas Day, he had taken the three children to live with him, never to be separated again.

A Fast Sled

I had nine brothers and sisters, and there wasn't a lot of money for new things. Living on a farm with that many siblings meant we found ways of having fun that didn't cost a lot. One was with an old commercial chicken building on our farm that had a low ground floor and a steep roof. The snow in the winter was always high enough that it packed up to the roof. The snow also covered the roof. This created a perfect sledding slope.

We didn't have money for sleds, but that didn't stop us. We found that the scoop shovels that we used to shovel grain would work. These were plentiful on our farm. We would sit on the shovel with the handle to the front. We would put our feet out front along the handle, or if we were really good at balancing, we could put our feet up on the handle and lean back. I started sledding down this roof by the time I was five years old.

I never saw any other sled until the time I was ten. I had joined the Cub Scouts, and we were going to the sand dunes.

I showed up carrying my scoop shovel.

"What's that?" Rod said with disgust.

"It's a scoop shovel," I replied.

"I can see that," Rod replied. "But why did you bring it sledding?"

I thought everyone used a scoop shovel for sledding, so I thought it was a dumb question. By this time, all the other boys had gathered around.

"This is what we use for sledding," I said.

Rod rolled his eyes. "That's the dumbest thing I ever heard."

I looked at the sleds the other boys were carrying. There was no one else with a scoop shovel. Theirs actually were sleds. Rod's was especially nice. It was a round saucer with curled-up edges.

We loaded into our Cub Scout leader's suburban and headed to the sledding hill. All the way there, the other boys continued to mock my scoop shovel.

"Where do you usually go sledding with your shovel?" Lenny asked.

I explained about the chicken building roof. They all laughed and said it was stupid.

When we got to the sledding hill, we hurried to the top. I quickly learned how nice the other boys' sleds were. They climbed on them and zipped down the hill. They didn't have to worry about balancing to not tip over. And even though my scoop worked well as a sled, it had far more drag. I only went about half as far as they did. They let me try their sleds, and I grew very unsatisfied with my scoop shovel.

My mother had volunteered to make hot chocolate for us, so our Cub Scout leader was taking us to my house. I was deeply considering how I could get a sled, when Rod mockingly said, "Maybe when we get to your house, we should try your sledding roof with a real sled."

The boys all thought that was a good idea. So, once we arrived at my home, while my mother prepared the hot chocolate, we boys headed out to the sledding roof. We climbed to the top, and I went down first to show them how I used the scoop shovel.

When I got back to the top, Rod said, "Now watch what a real sled will do."

He jumped on his sled, and when he reached the spot where I had stopped, he was still moving at high speed. One thing I hadn't thought about was that the big manure pit where the wet manure drained was in that direction. It was covered with a thin layer of snow.

I never worried about it because my shovel sled wouldn't go that far. But Rod's took him on top of it.

He stopped, turned to me, and laughed. "See what a good sled will do?"

He then stepped off of his sled and immediately dropped up to his neck in wet manure.

As the other boys gasped, I decided my scoop shovel sled was a good one after all.

Vote of Confidence

We attend a little country church in our rural community. I have been involved in many community events and have taken on lots of assignments that have come from the congregation leaders. Mostly, I have worked in scouting.

On Tuesday one week, I had been asked by the congregational leaders to take a new assignment with the young men. The announcement would be given in the church meeting on Sunday, and as usual, everyone in the congregation would be given a chance to either support or express their concern about the assignment. But as I was coming into the church that Sunday, one of the congregational leaders stopped me and told me they had changed their mind. They felt inspired to ask me instead to be the person who would teach the children music.

The members of our little country church have certain idiosyncrasies, and one of them is a strong distinction between what men do and what women do. A man teaching the children music would be like assigning him to play on a female sports team. But I had been taught by my father that if a call came from church leaders, a person should accept it, and heaven would help him overcome his inadequacies. So, with great apprehension, I accepted.

I wondered what the members of the congregation would say. I was particularly nervous about the assignment since my wife was a music major in college, and I didn't even know if I was on pitch half the time. The only thing going for me was that I loved children.

It would be a full week before it would be announced to the congregation. That just gave me more time to worry about it. I wondered what my children would think when they learned that their dad, who couldn't sing right half the time, would be teaching music. I talked to my wife about it, but we didn't mention anything to our children other than to tell them that I was getting an unusual assignment.

When the next week came, and the announcement was made, it went worse than I expected. Instead of the solemnity that usually exists with these announcements, the congregation burst into laughter, starting with my own children. It was to such an extent that the head congregational leader, whom we call "the bishop," had to pause the meeting for everyone to calm down. Once the laughter stopped, the meeting was restarted, only to have everyone once more burst into laughter. This time the bishop spoke to the congregation about how sometimes they, the leaders, felt directed to do unusual things.

No one expressed any concern about the assignment, so it was to officially start the next week. I thought it might be good for me to watch what the current music teacher did. But the minute I stepped into the children's meeting room, one of the ladies in charge handed me the songbook.

I shook my head and handed it back. "I don't start until next week. I just came to watch."

She shoved the book back to me. "We don't have anyone for you to watch, so get up and lead."

Nothing I said would change her mind, and she would not accept no for an answer, so I soon found myself trembling in front of forty children. We sang a song that I have known since I was a boy, but in my flustered state, I mixed half of one verse with half of another. I finally stopped the music.

"Maybe we should try that again," I said.

One little eight-year-old girl raised her hand. When I called on her, she asked, "Are you going to be our new music teacher?"

"Yes," I replied.

The little girl rolled her eyes. "That really stinks," she said. "You mess things up."

And with that, I thought, "I hope heaven has more confidence in me than I do."

A Group Rate

After a long day of work, Jay sat down to read the paper. The big headline was the news of Apollo 8. NASA had finally been able to have astronauts travel from the earth to the moon. Jay was sure it wouldn't be long before someone walked on the moon.

He was just getting into the news when his little daughter tugged on his sleeve.

"Daddy, can we go to a movie? We haven't been for a long time."

Jay looked up from his paper into the pleading face of his little daughter. "Sweetheart, I'd love for us to go, but there are a lot more of us now, and I'm not sure we can afford it."

Jay and his wife had always scraped money together to take their three daughters to a movie about once per month. But after his wife was gone, it was hard to keep everything in their lives together, let alone go to the movies. It had been a hard couple of years.

But then Jay met Helen, and they fell in love. Helen had six girls of her own, and when Jay considered the price of eleven tickets, it seemed almost impossible for them to afford that much. Movie tickets for those over twelve were three dollars, and tickets for those under twelve were two-fifty. He, his first wife, and their three girls cost almost fourteen dollars. With eleven people, it would be around thirty dollars. But as Jay looked into his little daughter's pleading face and thought about the tough years they had been through, he decided they all could use a trip to the movies.

"But there won't be any money left over for popcorn," he said.

They all loaded into the station wagon. That was the only vehicle they could afford that would haul eleven people. Some sat in the back without seats, and others had to sit on the older children's laps. This lack of good transportation had also meant that what family vacations they could afford had to be closer to home. No one wanted to travel very far with someone sitting on their lap.

When they arrived at the theater, the girls paired up. Helen was a good organizer. Each of the older girls was assigned to a younger one. That way, the smaller children had someone to watch out for them to keep them from getting lost. Helen took care of the youngest daughter herself.

As Jay and Helen, along with their nine daughters, walked the block to the theater, people stared. As they got closer to the theater, Jay laughed to himself when he saw the poster for what was showing. It was *Cheaper by the Dozen*. Maybe that was why they had received so many stares.

The children all stood patiently while Jay went to the window to pay.

"We have six over twelve and five under twelve," he told the lady.

She calculated and then said, "That will be eleven dollars."

Jay gasped. "Eleven dollars? I thought it would be three times that. I'm not complaining, but I don't want to cheat you, either."

"We have a special deal this month," the lady said. "All scout troops get in for one dollar per person, even the leaders. It doesn't matter whether it's a Boy Scout troop or whether it's a Girl Scout troop, like yours."

Jay smiled. "Actually, we aren't a Girl Scout troop. We're a blended family, and these are our daughters."

The lady pulled her glasses down to the end of her nose and looked down the line of nine girls. When she slid her glasses back into place, she smiled and spoke firmly. "It looks like a Girl Scout troop to me. That will be eleven dollars."

Jay paid for the tickets and thanked the lady.

The show title was right, he thought, and they even had money left over for popcorn.

At Any Price

Don's wife called out to him. "Don, the phone's for you."

Don picked up the receiver and said hello.

"Don," the man's voice on the line said, "this is Charles. You delivered a load of hay to me today."

"Yes," Don replied. "Is there a problem?"

"The hay is no good. My cows won't eat it. I'm not willing to pay more than fifty dollars per ton for it because that's just the way cows are about bad hay."

Don gasped. "Fifty dollars! But we agreed on one hundred and fifty, and that was a good price for you with what most hay is going for right now."

"Well, I can't pay you that much if the cows won't eat it," Charles said.

Don took a deep breath and tried to consider what to do.

While Don was thinking, Charles continued. "I will have a check out to you tomorrow."

"I haven't agreed to that," Don said. "I will need to think about it and get back to you."

When Don's wife walked in, she asked, "What was that all about?"

Don told her the story. When he finished, he said, "Hay prices almost everywhere are more than a hundred and seventy-five per ton. I was giving him a good deal at one-fifty."

"Does he usually cheat people?" Don's wife asked.

"I don't know," Don replied. "It's my first time dealing with him."

Don decided to call some other farmers to see what they could tell him about Charles. One old, retired farmer said he had been in the very same situation with Charles.

"What did you do?" Don asked.

"There wasn't much I could do. It's a long way out to his place, and we used his tractor to unload the hay. He wasn't about to let me use it to load it up and take it away."

The more Don thought about it, the madder it made him. Besides, hay was scarce, and prices were still climbing. He probably could have sold it for more, but Charles had talked him down. Don finally made a decision.

He called his son and asked him if he could take the next day off from work. "I'll pay you to work for me," Don told him.

Don loaded his tractor on the flatbed trailer. The next day, bright and early, with Don in the semi and his son in the pickup pulling the trailer with the tractor on it, they were on their way to Charles's farm. They arrived mid-morning. Charles was nowhere to be seen, just as Don had hoped. Don quickly loaded the hay back onto his truck. Charles had fed part of one bale, so Don loaded what was left of it into the back of his pickup. Don and his son were soon on their way back home.

That night, Don received an angry phone call from Charles.

"What in the devil's name am I supposed to feed my cows?" Charles asked.

"That's not my problem," Don said.

Charles hung up angrily. But a few days later, he called back and was humbler.

"I'm willing to pay you the full one hundred and fifty for your bad hay," Charles said. "I can't find any anywhere else."

Don had expected the call might come. Farmers share information with each other when someone tries to cheat them. Besides, most of the hay in the valley was already sold.

"I've already sold it at two hundred per ton," Don said. "It goes out tomorrow."

"But we had a deal," Charles said, hotly.

"We did, and you broke it," Don replied.

"I'll pay you two-hundred and five a ton," Charles said. "I've just got to have some hay."

"Sorry," Don replied. "If your cows won't eat it at one-fifty per ton, they won't eat it at any price."

Everyone knows that's just the way cows are.

A Ring of Dough

Sandra laughed. "What could possibly go wrong when making bread?"

I grew up on a farm pretty much in the middle of nowhere. One of the things I learned well was the value of self-sufficiency. And when I was leaving for two years to serve a mission in New York, my mother insisted that I spend time learning to cook the main foods we usually ate.

When I got to New York, I spent a lot of time helping struggling families. Much of their struggle was financial, and self-sufficiency skills can help a person save money.

When the ladies of the church congregation learned that I made home-made bread, they asked if I would do a demonstration for all who were interested. I felt awkward teaching women how to cook and said so. That was when Sandra, the president of the women, assured me it would be okay. She also promised to provide all the ingredients that I needed.

Sandra told me the group wouldn't be too big. "There will probably be about a half dozen women there, and we are going to also invite their husbands to enjoy the fresh home-made bread. We'll also allow the women to invite friends, but I doubt more than one or two extras will come."

When I arrived at the church the night of the demonstration, two tables were set up for people to sit at and eat, and another two were there for us to knead the bread. Sandra had all the needed supplies in the kitchen. But as the time for the demonstration approached, we were in for a surprise as the hall started to fill. More tables were set up, and by the time the demonstration was to start, more than fifty women were there with almost an equal number of men.

Sandra sent her assistant to the store for more supplies and bread pans. We decided one loaf of bread could feed about four people, so we would need more than twenty-five loaves. The women organized in groups of two, and together they did all the things I showed them while their husbands hungrily watched. The women mixed the dough and kneaded it. They seemed to enjoy punching and rolling the dough. We put it into the pans, and then we moved the pans to the kitchen to let the bread rise while some women provided some musical entertainment.

Once the entertainment was over, the loaves had risen and were tall and beautiful. It was time to start running them through the ovens. That was the moment when one of the ladies realized she was missing her wedding ring. It was obvious it had to be in one of the loaves, but they were all in identical pans. Hoping to save as many loaves as possible, the women went through the loaves one at a time. As fate would have it, the ring was in the very last loaf.

The loaves were put back in the pans, but they never rise well a second time. The entertainment did a half-hearted second rendition of the same music, and then the half-risen loaves were put into the four ovens. When they came out, people ate with gusto, but I knew the loaves were heavy and flat.

One old man said to me, "They were good and all, don't get me wrong, but I think we'll stick to store-bought bread."

As the man walked away, Sandra, who had heard what he had said, came up and put her hand on my arm. "This is my fault. I guess I now understand what can go wrong."

Then she smiled and said, "I guess we'll just have to do it again. But next time, we'll have everyone remove their wedding rings first."

Gender Differences

With Valentine's Day approaching, I have thought quite a bit about the differences in the genders. Watching boys and girls in my classes at the university, I see those differences quite often, and they make me smile. Of course, I had already seen them between my wife, Donna, and me. But often it's more pronounced among young people.

As an example, one day a girl came into class. She apparently had gotten a haircut, though to me, it looked the same as it did in our previous class. But, the other girls in her group noticed the difference immediately.

"Wow!" one girl said. "You got a haircut."

"Yes," the first girl replied. "And now I can't do anything with it. It doesn't lay right on the left side, and the flair is wrong in the back."

She then went on for about five minutes, describing in minute detail how bad it was. When she finally finished, one of the girls in her group said, "Well, I think it's cute."

All the other girls in the group voiced their agreement.

A few minutes later, just about the time class was to start, a boy came in. He obviously had a haircut because, compared to the previous class day, his hair was almost nonexistent. He sat down, and the boy closest to him noticed his hair.

"Hey, dude, you got a haircut," the boy said.

"Yeah," the boy with the haircut replied.

"Man, it's ugly," the first boy said.

"Yeah," the boy with the haircut replied.

There was no long, detailed explanation of it, no concern on how it laid, nothing. It was just ugly.

Another big difference is how boys and girls ask each other out.

When I was younger, girls almost never asked a boy out, but now it's apparently quite acceptable. And watching the differences is interesting.

A boy will try to ask a girl out quietly. But when a girl offers an invitation to a boy, it's pretty much a community event. The girl will often have a whole entourage of her friends accompany her, surround the boy, and do whatever it takes to make it the social activity of the year.

I have analyzed these differences and have come to a few conclusions. A boy is afraid the girl will turn him down, so he does it quietly just in case, to reduce the humiliation. At first, I thought the girl did it in a big group so the boy would be too embarrassed to turn her down. But I've since come to the conclusion that I'm thinking like a man. From watching these episodes, I now feel the girl tends to have a great desire to have the boy be proud of her, so she wants everyone to see it when he says yes.

Of course, I seldom see a boy turn a girl down in that situation. There is nothing like enduring the wrath of a whole group of girls, and the boy knows it, or quickly will. So, I suppose if her purpose is to guarantee that he will say yes, that tends to work as well.

As for myself and Donna, I realize those differences are still there. She was a thousand miles away visiting our new granddaughter. She called and told me she found a beautiful coat that she wanted to buy for me.

"I want to send you a picture to see if you like it," she said.

"How much does it cost?" I asked.

"I want to have you see a picture first to decide if you like it before I tell you," she replied.

"If you tell me how much it costs, I can tell you if I like it even without a picture," I said.

I could tell by her sigh that she thought I was thinking too much like a man. But when she told me the price, I knew I didn't like it.

Seriously, I saved her lots of time sending the picture.

Capture the Flag

February is Scout Month, and it always brings back fond memories of my time as a scoutmaster. We live near a lot of wonderful natural beauty, and we spent a lot of time camping.

One particular winter weekend, my assistant, Rod, and I took fourteen boys and went camping down by the river. Nights are long and days are short in the winter, so there weren't a lot of hours of light left by the time we reached the campsite. The boys were planning a big game of capture the flag.

"There are about two hours of daylight left," I told them. "If you hurry and set up camp, you could have most of it to play."

"Setting up camp is boring," Gordy complained. "Why don't we play capture the flag first?"

"Because you won't get camp set up," I said. "We've been there before, and that's why we have the rules we do. Just work fast."

My encouragement seemed to fall on deaf ears. For the next couple of hours, I heard nothing but complaining while the light faded quickly away.

I had food ready to eat long before they finished setting up the camp. When we finished eating, we had to clean up before they could do anything else. Again, they spent more time complaining than working. We just finished when the moon came out, and it was beautiful. It reflected on the snow and made the evening about as light as the early part of a sunrise.

"I know," Mort said, "let's do a moonlight game of capture the flag."

"And when we get done," Devin said, "we can tell ghost stories around the campfire."

I didn't relish the thought of being up most of the night trying to make sure the boys stayed out of trouble, but I had an idea.

"If you guys expect me to tell ghost stories, we probably better do it first."

Rod looked at me and smiled as if he knew I had something up my sleeve. The boys told a few mildly scary stories, then it was my turn. I didn't know many ghost stories. The boys thought I did, but I always made them up as I went along. I was just about to start when we heard a coyote howl. Then we heard another, and another. Though the coyotes weren't foolish enough to come near our camp, the boys joked about it.

One boy smacked another one. "I bet you'll be too chicken to play capture the flag, now."

I could see the perfect opening, so I started my story. "Years ago, there was a group of scouts who decided to play capture the flag in the middle of the night. There were fourteen of them. They had heard the coyotes howl, but coyotes aren't that big, so no one was scared. But the scoutmaster said, 'I'm not sure that's a coyote. Listen to the way the sound seems to come from all directions at once, and it's deep, growly, and eerie.'

"But the boys didn't listen. None of them wanted to be thought of as chicken. They set up their flags, a blue one on one end, and a red one on the other. As they played, the coyote sound continued echoing all around them and grew louder. The scoutmaster was sitting by the fire, and he realized that the shouts from the boys had faded away, and the coyote sound had disappeared. He wondered if the boys had gone to bed.

"He took his flashlight and went to see where the boys were. They weren't in their tents. He found no boys, but he did find the flags, each torn into seven strips, flapping from the trees. He searched all night, and he didn't see any sign of the boys, but he did see fourteen pairs of fire-red eyes staring at him from the brush.

"The next morning, he found prints that looked like human hands, with long claws at the end of the fingers."

Mort's voice quivered as he asked, "What kind of prints were they?"

"All I know," I replied, "is that werewolves are supposed to make that kind of track."

Gordy yawned and stretched. "You know, guys, I'm really tired. What say we go to bed and play capture the flag tomorrow?"

They all readily agreed, and soon the camp was quiet, except for Rod's chuckling and the howl of coyotes in the distance.

Wrestling Dilemma

February always reminds me of wrestling. That was the month for district and state tournaments when I was young. I remember one wrestling experience well.

In the fall of my senior year, wrestling had just started when the girl I had dated for a little while came to talk to me. Sheila was a junior, and her love was journalism. She was one of the main reporters for the school newspaper. What made her stand out from most other students working on the school paper was that there was little she wouldn't do to get a good story.

"Daris," she said, "can I talk to you?"

"Sure," I replied. "What do you want to talk about?"

"I think I want to join the wrestling team."

There were no girls on the wrestling team. So if this had been anyone else, I might have been surprised. But I had learned long ago that Sheila was anything but predictable.

"Why would you want to do that?" I asked.

"I want to do a story about what it's like to be a girl on the wrestling team. What do you think of that?"

"Personally, I think that's a crazy reason to go out for wrestling or any sport. A person should do it only because they want to compete."

"Well, maybe I think I can compete. Maybe I could even beat you."

I thought she was joking, and I smiled. But she apparently wasn't, because she became agitated with me.

"You think it's funny?" she asked, hotly. "Maybe I could even beat you. I used to wrestle against my brother, and he was a varsity wrestler."

"Okay," I said. "Do it if you want to."

"What would you do if I wrestled you?" she asked.

"You wouldn't," I replied. "I outweigh you by almost double, so we wouldn't even be close to the same weight class."

"But what if I did wrestle you? Would you treat me differently than another opponent and go easy on me?"

"No," I said. "If you wrestled me, you had better plan to compete hard."

I don't know what she thought of my answer, because she strode away. But word quickly got around about her plan, and my teammates teased me.

At lunch, Sheila informed me she would be at wrestling practice with another girl she had convinced to come with her. The more I tried to talk Sheila out of it, the more determined she became.

Finally, I said, "Okay. It's your choice."

"Would you hurt either of us if we wrestled you?" she asked.

I was offended by the question. "Of course not. At least not on purpose. I have never hurt an opponent on purpose. I have accidentally hurt some who were not prepared for the intensity of the sport. You just better be prepared to compete."

When I got to wrestling practice, the girls weren't there, but all the talk was of them. The coach was not pleased about the situation, afraid the girls would get hurt. But due to Title IX, they could join if they desired.

It was during our first break that Sheila and her friend showed up carrying gym bags. The sweat was pouring off us wrestlers as we came from the wrestling room, heading for the water fountain.

The two girls looked at us, and Sheila's friend asked her, "Will we be touching them? They are so sweaty and gross."

I looked at the girl with her perfect hair and clothes, and I laughed. "You'll get used to it. You'll be just as sweaty and gross."

Sheila's friend turned and walked out the door. Sheila poked me in the chest.

"Okay, so I'm not wrestling. But not because I'm scared to try. It's just because you're so . . . so . . . sweaty and disgusting!" And with that, she left to join her friend.

I already knew that I was sweaty and disgusting, but at least I wouldn't have to worry about dating a girl who was a teammate.

What Students Learned in Math Class, 2018

Over the years, we have found that one of the students' greatest criticisms of any math class is their claim that they didn't learn anything. Therefore, as part of their final, I have the students list ten things that they have learned. These items can be anything at all in relation to the class. They are allowed to write their list ahead of time and bring it to the final if they want. Most observations are quite normal, but some make for interesting reading. Each year, I list some of them, and here is this year's list. I haven't shared any for a while, so I thought it was about time again.

1) I learned that I really don't want to be a math major like I thought I did.

2) Math for the real world makes me afraid to go out into the real world.

3) I learned that my backpack is way too big to be practical.

4) I learned a lot more about taxes. I will still have my dad do them since he is an accountant, but I learned what he is doing when he does them.

5) I learned that in math, the calculator is man's best friend, not a dog.

6) Just being smart doesn't always help you in every class. Sometimes, you have to work.

7) I learned that no one in my apartment knows how to help me with math.

8) I learned that I am glad I am majoring in business.

9) I learned that taxes are complicated, so I am glad my fiancé is an accountant.

10) I learned that college math requires you to actually think.

11) I learned we work better in our group if someone actually knows

what they are doing.

12) I learned that I am stressed over everything when I procrastinate.

13) I learned how big of an ego the kid next to me has. He thinks he is top of the world.

14) I learned that Professor Howard is pretty cool about having people over to his house to milk his cow.

15) I learned that six girls living in an apartment creates a lot of tension and makes it hard to think in class.

16) I learned that girls need lots of compliments, or they can become angry cavewomen. *(Written by a boy.)*

17) If you pay attention, you will find out that Professor Howard actually has an awesome sense of humor. But a lot of people never know it.

18) It is hard to do all your homework for an entire chapter the day before the test.

19) If you do your homework before the test instead of after, it helps your grade... A LOT!

20) Sleep during the night and stay awake in class; you'll be surprised by what your teacher covers.

21) This semester I learned that I really hate when people waste my time, especially when they act like they know what they are doing when in reality, they don't. (This is talking about tutors, not you, Professor Howard.)

22) I learned that when a girl says hi to you when the two of you walk past each other, and then she turns around to say hi again, she is really saying she wants you to get her number.

23) I learned that Professor Howard was a collegiate athlete. I saw his picture in an old yearbook. Who would have guessed? He sure doesn't look like it now.

A Little Bit Out of It

Dora and Frank were some older neighbors that I often visited. They lived in a little trailer house. In the winter, I would haul wood from their shed and stack it by their door to make it more convenient for them to keep their house warm.

One winter day when I arrived, they weren't home. That was a little bit unusual because they seldom went anywhere in the winter. But I didn't think too much about it. I figured they must have gone to the store or something.

I set to work refilling their wood supply. I also shoveled their walk and chipped off the ice. Just as I was finishing and preparing to leave, another neighbor stopped to visit with me.

"You've heard that Dora's in the hospital, haven't you?" he asked.

"No," I replied. "What's the problem?"

"She had an allergic reaction to something," he said.

I decided I would pay Dora and Frank a visit at the hospital, but I was too dirty and sweaty to go directly there. I hurried home and showered and changed. I then drove to the hospital.

When I arrived, I checked in at the front desk, and they told me where Dora was. I went to her room and knocked on the open door. Frank, a man of few words, beckoned to me to come in. Dora greeted me, and we visited briefly before the doctor came in.

He told Frank the hospital needed to run some more tests, and Frank nodded. But when the doctor started to visit with Dora, she appeared frightened.

"Dora," the doctor said, "it's time to take you upstairs."

Suddenly, Dora started to yell. "No! No! I don't want to go!"

She tried to get up, almost ripping the I.V. from her arm. The doctor stopped her, but not without great effort. He hit the nurse-call button to get additional help. A nurse appeared and joined in the fray, but Nora was fighting like a lion. They called for more help. Frank and I moved out of the way as another nurse and an orderly came in. It took all of them great effort to keep Dora from escaping.

The doctor asked Frank if they could give Dora a sedative to calm her, and Frank nodded. With a quick shot into her IV, Dora finally settled down and was soon asleep. That was when they took her for some more tests. I said goodbye to Frank as he headed to the elevator with them.

The next day, after work, I went to the hospital to see how Dora was doing. Frank nodded a hello as I came in. Dora was sitting up eating her dinner.

"So, how are you doing today?" I asked her.

Dora shoved her food to the side. "I think I need to explain about yesterday," she said.

"Only if you want to," I replied.

"The thing is," she said, "when you came, I was still a little out of it from my allergic reaction. And when you come to visit us, it's almost always in our home. So, as we sat there visiting, I somehow got the idea I was at home.

"Then, as we visited, the doctor came in, and I couldn't figure out who he was or why he was in my home dressed in white. But then when he said he was going to take me upstairs, my mind reminded me that our trailer didn't have an upstairs. And as I sat there staring at him, in his white robe, it came to my mind that the upstairs he was talking about was heaven. I was sure he was the angel of death, and he had come for me."

I laughed. "Dora, as hard as you fought, the angel of death would have had his hands full taking you. It's too bad you weren't entered in Olympic wrestling."

Frank smiled and said some of the few words I'd ever heard him say. He said, "She could have won the gold."

The Violin

I went to the high school orchestra concert and visited with people before it started. When the lights dimmed, we all moved to our seats and quieted down. The youth came filing in, and the audience applauded. As the young musicians moved to their designated chairs, I smiled as I saw who the senior boy was who took the concertmaster chair.

Nathan was a big, muscular boy who looked like he should have been a linebacker for a football team, not playing violin in an orchestra. But Nathan's orchestra story started many years earlier.

He was always a big boy for his age, and everyone expected him to play football. The school had one of the best teams in the state, having won the state championship many times. Those on the football team were quite popular in the school. So, when Nathan got into fifth grade, everyone was surprised when he didn't try out for football. That was when the teasing started. Most of it was in fun, but some of it was downright mean. It continued to the point that he finally decided to join one of the teams. And because of his size, he was fairly good, but he wasn't as outstanding as many people thought he should be.

Nathan's mother was the secretary in our department. In high school, I had been an all-conference and all-state football lineman, so Nathan's mother thought it would be good to have him talk to me. She felt that maybe I could motivate him. But when he came to me, I could sense something was wrong.

"Do you like football?" I asked.

He shrugged. "It's okay."

"Just okay?"

He shrugged again, and we started to talk. I learned that Nathan was not really interested in football. His real love was music—classical music, no less.

"Have you told your mother?" I asked.

He shook his head. "Everyone just expects me to play football."

"I think she would understand," I said. "Everyone expected my children to do sports. But when they tried, their hearts weren't in it. If your heart isn't in it, you will never excel. You need to do what you love to do, not what others say you should do."

For the next few days, our department secretary was not her jovial self, and I wondered if I had been wrong in what I said. She wouldn't say what was bothering her, but we could all tell something was on her mind.

It was about this time that one of my colleagues came to my office. His wife was the orchestra teacher at the middle school. He told me he wanted to talk about Nathan.

"Daris," he said, "I don't know if you know, but Nathan wants to play violin in the orchestra. But since his mother is a single parent, she doesn't have the money to get him a violin. Would you consider donating?"

I smiled. "Gladly."

There were only twelve members of our department, but we collected enough money to buy Nathan a high-quality, professional violin. A few days later, our department members gathered in the department foyer, and my colleague presented the beautiful instrument to Nathan's mother. She cried openly as she accepted the gift for her son. And she was again her jovial self.

Nathan loved orchestra, and he excelled. It wasn't long before he was the lead violinist. Though some people still teased him about not playing football, his musical talent was soon recognized, and the teasing faded away.

So now, as I watched Nathan play, including a phenomenal

solo, I thought of how important it is to do the thing you love the most. But I also thought about how grateful I was for the good people I worked with who were willing to support a young man when he needed it most.

A Difference in Culture

I was nineteen years old and living in New York when I first met Juan. His family had come to the United States from South America, and he was proud of his heritage. He was a pleasant young man and a jokester. But one thing he especially liked to do was to challenge the rest of us to see who could eat the hottest, spiciest foods.

Juan would eat a hot pepper and say, "Where I live, we eat chili peppers like you eat M&Ms."

Of course, living in Buffalo, New York, the most famous spicy food was Buffalo Chicken Wings. Juan issued a challenge to the rest of us, claiming he could eat hotter chicken wings than anyone, and he dared us to prove otherwise. In our group of a dozen young men, four decided to take the challenge.

There were a few places in Buffalo, all of which claimed to be the restaurant that first made chicken wings. Juan told the challengers to choose whichever one they wanted.

One of the challengers, Donaldson, chose a restaurant based on its hotness factor. This restaurant claimed to have chicken wings from super-super mild to what they called "hot death." On a day off from work, the twelve of us went there to eat and watch the challenge.

Though most of us didn't plan to be part of the competition, we thought we would see how far up the hotness scale we could go. We started by ordering a platter of the super-super mild. We each ate one. They were barely spicy, and I liked them. We ordered a super mild next. This burned slightly for me, and some of our group went no hotter. Next was the mild. When I tried that, tears rolled from my eyes, and I decided I was happy to end there.

Most of us quit at that level, but the four challengers and Juan kept going. But as the temperature increased, one by one the challengers, eyes watering, dropped out. There were still three heat levels left when the last challenger conceded victory to Juan. As each person reached their hottest level, there would be lots of gulping of pop or anything to try to wash away the burn, and Juan would point at the person and say, "Gringo," and laugh.

After the last challenger dropped out, all pitched in and bought a platter of "hot death," and Juan, to our great admiration, ate every wing on it.

Juan's victory was the talk of our meetings for about a week. Then, one day, Donaldson received a package from home. In it was a note from his mother to share it with all of us. It was full of cookies, and something else that Donaldson said was his favorite treat. There were twelve small vials of sweetened cinnamon and a package of toothpicks. Donaldson showed us that he loved to dip the toothpick into the cinnamon and then lick it.

We each took our cinnamon and followed his lead. It was really good, and soon we were all licking our cinnamon toothpicks. But that was when something interesting happened. Juan licked his the first time, and his eyes grew wide, and he started to scream. He rushed to the kitchen sink and started gulping water and trying to rinse his mouth. Finally, he turned to us.

"You tricked me!"

"It's just cinnamon oil," Donaldson said, dipping a toothpick and licking it off.

Juan walked over to Donaldson and jerked the bottle from his hand. He picked up a new toothpick, dipped it in the cinnamon, and licked it. Again, his eyes grew wide, and he screamed and ran to the kitchen sink. He still thought it was a trick, so after Donaldson showed him again, and licked off a toothpick, Juan grabbed the toothpick out of Donaldson's mouth, and to our disgust, licked it, too. Once more, we watched Juan scream and run to the sink.

"It must just be a difference of spices that we are used to in our culture," I said.

When Juan finally pulled his mouth away from the water faucet, Donaldson pointed at him and said, "Non-Gringo," and we all laughed.

So, Donaldson had an extra container of cinnamon for himself, and Juan never teased us again.

The Blind Date

I was in college, and though I was a good athlete, I was also shy, and I didn't date much. It was hard for me to think of any reason a girl would want to go out with me.

One day, a girl from the church I attended called and asked to talk to me. Deanna was a beautiful girl, and everyone liked her. All of my roommates were sure they were madly in love with her. So, I couldn't imagine why she would want to talk to me.

"Daris," she said, "a sorority dinner and dance is coming up on April 1st, and a girl I know needs a date. Would you go with her?"

I didn't need to check my empty social calendar to tell her I was available.

"I'd love to go, but I'm not very good at dancing or social things. Are you sure she wouldn't rather go with one of my roommates?"

"I'm sure. She knows about you, and she's excited. But she may not be the best looking."

"I can't claim that I am, either," I replied. "And if she's willing to go with me, I'd be happy to be her date. I just don't want her to expect somebody too exciting."

"You'll be wonderful," Deanna said. "I know you'll treat her well. That's why I asked you."

Deanna told me a little more about the girl and that her name was DeeDee. When I hung up, my roommates gathered around. Bryce, who had answered the phone, had already told everyone it was Deanna.

"What did she want?" Bryce asked.

"She asked me to the sorority dinner and dance," I said.

"She asked you, the king of I-can't-dance?" Bryce asked, incredulously. "She could choose anyone. Why would she choose you?"

"I'm not her date," I replied. "I'm going with a friend of hers."

"Oh, a blind date," David said. "Those can be disastrous. And if the girl needs someone else to ask for her, she probably needs help."

"Well, it's not like I'm the most socially adept, either," I replied.

"You've got a good point there," Bryce said.

As the day grew closer, I became more nervous. The girl sounded like a great girl, and I hoped she wouldn't be disappointed when she met me. It seemed way too soon that I was dressed in my best suit and on my way to Deanna's apartment. When I arrived, I stood there for most of a minute, taking deep breaths to calm my nerves. Finally, I knocked on the door.

A girl with frizzy, uncombed hair, wearing a month's supply of poorly placed makeup, answered. Her dress had probably been nice when it was new, but it definitely needed ironing.

She smiled a crooked smile and said, "Hi, I'm DeeDee."

I held out my hand. "Hi, I'm Daris."

The girl burst out laughing, and I felt confused. Was my name funny? Then, from behind the door, Deanna and a bunch of other girls all came out dressed in beautiful gowns. They were all laughing, too, and they yelled, "April Fools!"

I was still confused. Deanna said, "We had Julie dress up and pretend to be your date."

"Oh," I said. "So, I don't really have a date?"

Suddenly, the girls all went quiet and looked at each other.

Deanna took my hand. "Daris, I'm your date. DeeDee is my nickname."

"I'm going with you? But my roommates said you could go with anyone you wanted."

She squeezed my hand a little tighter and smiled. "And I am. I want to go with you because I like you, and I've seen how respectful and kind you are to us girls at church."

All night I struggled to believe that Deanna would want me to be her date. But I had a wonderful time. The food was excellent, and the dancing was fun.

When the evening ended, I walked home, almost in a daze. When I came in, my roommates gathered to hear about my date.

"What was she like?" Bryce asked.

"My date was actually Deanna," I said.

My roommates all looked at each other, then burst out laughing.

"Nice try," Bryce said. "But we know it's April Fools' Day."

I smiled and realized I couldn't convince them otherwise, so I didn't try.

I've Seen Worse

My daughter asked me if I would judge at a debate tournament.

"I've never even been to a debate tournament," I replied.

"It's okay," she said. "They'll train you. Besides, the most important part of judging is to give the students information about what you feel they can do better. If you just give them points and don't say why you scored them the way you did, it will mean nothing."

She said every student was asked to provide a judge for one of the tournaments, and I could choose which one I went to. I looked at the tournament schedule and determined one that would work for me.

On the appointed day, I went to the designated high school. All the judges met in one room, and we were given some training. By the time I received my first assignment, I still felt totally unprepared.

For my first judging round, the students helped me understand what was supposed to happen. I found both teams to be quite equal, but I also found little suggestions that I could share with them to help them know what they could do to improve. I wrote quite a lot of notes on their papers both during and after the debate.

I judged a second round with similar results. I found I enjoyed it more than I thought I would.

Eventually, I had a break and went to the judges' lounge. The debate team parents of that school provided some taco salads for the judges. I started to fill a plate, and the lady who was serving asked how the judging was going.

"This is my first time," I said. "I think it's going okay, but I have nothing to compare against."

"Well, I've judged a lot of these," she said, "and I've seen worse, but not too much worse."

Since I was the last person in line, she quit serving and filled a plate of food for herself. She came over to the table I was at, and three other ladies joined us as well. The first lady continued to talk about how bad the debaters were.

"In the judging I have done," she said, "I have seldom seen such poor performances."

"Well," another lady said, "you've got to realize that for some of these kids, it's the first time they have ever tried this."

No matter how much others tried to turn the conversation to a positive tone, the first lady kept sharing her negative comments. Suddenly, I bit into something that was really chewy. I tried to chew my way through it, but it didn't get any smaller, and it hooked on my teeth. Finally, I spit it onto my fork and set it on the plate. I tried to do it inconspicuously, but the lady next to me noticed.

"What is that?" she asked.

I picked it up and carefully analyzed it. "I think it's a rubber band," I said. "One of the bigger kind that someone wears on their braces."

Another lady at the table just about gagged. She swallowed a few times to keep her food down and then set her fork down and pushed her food away.

The lady who had been so negative started to apologize. "Oh, I'm so sorry. I have no idea how that got in there."

"It's no big deal," I said, and I continued eating.

"No big deal!" the lady who almost lost her meal said. "You found a rubber band like that in your food, and you say it's no big deal? And how can you continue eating?"

Looking right at the lady who had been complaining about the debate students, I laughed and said, "I'm a scoutmaster. I've seen worse."

The lady smiled an embarrassed smile and never said another word of complaint.

Teaching Children to Read

I was a new father, and I wanted to do everything right. When I would come across an article that said what a father should do, I always read it. So when I learned that children who were read to when they were young tended to read sooner and better, I was determined to put it into practice. The article also said that a child who learned to read at a young age would then have a much bigger advantage in school and in life. Further, it claimed even a baby was soothed hearing parents read to them.

My first child, a daughter, was only a few weeks old when I decided to implement this. I was in college at the time studying mathematics. I had to do a lot of reading, so why not give it a shot? I took her in my arms and started reading to her about calculus and Newton. It didn't seem to soothe her at all. In fact, she became fussier.

My wife suggested that maybe math isn't the most soothing thing in the world. She bought a bunch of children's books at a second-hand store for me. I started reading these to our daughter, and she did seem to like them better. It never took too long before she was asleep.

I continued to do this as my other children came along. In the evening, just before bedtime, my children would gather around, and I would read to them. I tried to use a different voice for every character, and we had a lot of fun.

Then, when my oldest daughter turned four, I decided it was time to start teaching her letters so she could read on her own. I was afraid that she might start behind in kindergarten as I did when I started school in first grade. All my children were reading by the time they went to school.

My oldest son seemed the most fascinated about learning. When I started teaching his sister, who was just older than he was, he would climb on my lap and try to say the letters before she could. He knew all the letters before he was four, and not long afterward, he could read basic books. By the time he went to kindergarten, his favorite series was *The Hardy Boys*.

I never thought there could be anything bad about a child learning to read early, but one day, I received a call from my son's upset kindergarten teacher.

"You need to have a talk with your son!" she said.

"What has he done?" I asked.

"When a child does something really good or really bad, I write a note to their parents and pin it to them," she replied. "But when they get on the bus, they take their notes off and have your son read them. If the notes are bad, the children throw them away. I've even tried to write in cursive, but he has figured out how to read that, too. We know this must be happening because we are finding all the bad notes in the garbage can on the bus."

"Maybe the problem isn't my son," I said. "It seems wrong to send a 'kill the messenger' note home with the messenger."

She didn't like that much and insisted I talk to him. So I did have a talk with him, but I'm not sure the practice totally ended. The other kids were paying him candy, nickels, dimes, and other valuable childhood things to read the notes. He viewed it more like a part-time job and couldn't see any real reason he shouldn't continue. Though no one could prove it, I think the children just became more covert about it.

But I do know that when I went to the parent-teacher conference, there was an unusually high number of parents who were surprised at some of the naughty things their children had been doing, even though the teacher said she had sent home notes about it.

A Health Record

Ann's daughter, Sheila, was getting married, and there were a million things to do before the wedding. There was a wedding cake to order, catering to set up, and lots of bridesmaid dresses to sew. The list went on and on, and there was only a week left to do it. So, when Sheila approached Ann one morning with a simple request, it was almost overwhelming.

"Mom," Sheila said, "I need to go to the doctor for a premarital exam. Dennis needs the car, so could you take me when you go to town?'

Ann looked at the sewing pile and sighed. The problem with doctor appointments is they are never predictable. A person might get right in, and they might be an hour or more—time that Ann didn't have.

"I'll tell you what," Ann said, "I'll take you to the doctor's office and drop you off. I'll run all my errands, and then I'll come back. Hopefully, you will be done with your checkup, and I can just come in and pay the bill."

Sheila thought that was a good idea, so after breakfast, they both headed to town. Ann dropped Sheila off and then went to the catering store. She also picked up some more fabric and ordered the cake. She was gone long enough that she was sure Sheila would be done with her appointment. But when Ann walked into the doctor's office, she found Sheila was waiting for her.

"Mom, I'm glad you're here. I haven't had my appointment yet because I'm supposed to fill out this paperwork first, and I don't know all the answers. I've filled out the stuff about me, but I need some family information."

Ann looked at the papers that Sheila had and saw there were

about five pages. Sheila had done the first two, but the others were still blank.

"Has anyone in our family had any allergic reactions to painkillers?" Sheila asked.

Ann sighed as she took a seat and answered Sheila's question. Sheila marked the answer and then asked another question and then another. It took almost ten minutes to finish one page, and there were still a couple of pages to go. Ann could feel her tension level rising as she thought about all the things she had to do. Then suddenly, she had an interesting thought.

Ann got up and walked to the receptionist station. "Can you tell me what all these questions on this form are for?"

"Sure," the receptionist replied. "They are to help with genetic issues when she has children. It will make it possible for us to help her with any family medical traits she has and will pass on to her children."

"This is just a big waste of time," Ann said in frustration. "You need to just do the checkup and forget all this."

The receptionist didn't seem to like that.

"We have our rules," she said, "and everyone has to fill out the family history for the premarital checkup. Why do you think you should be exempt from having to do it?"

"Because she's adopted and it's useless to her," Ann said.

Sheila was quickly ushered back for her checkup.

"Sorry, Mom," Sheila said sheepishly. "I didn't even think about that."

Ann smiled and felt her heart calm and her tension lift slightly as she hugged her daughter. "It's okay, and it's actually a good thing. You have been our little girl for so long, it is like you have always been our daughter. And I needed to be reminded that you are more important than dresses or cakes or anything else."

A Kitten's Mother

A friend and her family came out to our area this summer to enjoy the eclipse, and they came out to our house for a cookout. Our friend has some sweet children, and while they were at our house, the children fell in love with our kittens.

"They are old enough for us to give away, now," I told her.

She frowned. "Don't you dare tell my children. The last thing we need is another kitten. One of our dogs died, and they have already been begging for another pet."

But I didn't need to tell the children. While they were at our house, they carried the kittens everywhere. They played with the kittens, fed them, and never went far from them. I knew it would only be a matter of time until they asked. I was right. Before they left, I heard the begging.

"Mom, please!" they said over and over.

But their mother was adamant. "When we travel, we have to get someone to take care of the animals or take them someplace. We want to be free to go when we want to without having the bother."

Our friend won out that evening. Through all the pleading, she stayed strong, and the children left with no kitten. But a few days later, when they were leaving for home, they came back to our house. The children had finally worn her down. In fact, they had talked her into two kittens so that one wouldn't be lonely.

One kitten would be the responsibility of the eldest son, who was allowed to choose first because it was his dog that had died. The other would be the choice of the six-year-old daughter and her brother just older than her, since the other two children already had a dog. Before they left, our friend wanted to emphasize to the children the responsibility.

"These kittens are still small, barely old enough to leave their mother. If you take one, you will become their new mother. Are you willing to do that?"

All her children said they would, but our friend especially wanted a commitment from her six-year-old daughter.

The little girl looked up at her mother with her big happy eyes and said, "Yes, Momma. I will be just like a mother to it."

We gave them some kitten food and boxes to carry their new pets in for the long trip, and they headed home.

A few days later, our friend emailed me. The children wanted to know when the kittens were born so they could celebrate their birthday. My wife and I approximated it based on when we had seen the mother cat fat and when we hadn't.

Our friend's husband posted on Facebook occasionally to let us know how the kittens were growing and how much they were loved. But at Christmas, I got a special letter with extra info.

Apparently, our friend's six-year-old wanted to be the best mother to the kitten she could. But what does a mother cat do to take care of her kittens? The older siblings suggested she watch YouTube videos. A person can learn anything there.

So, sometime after they had taken the kittens home, our friend came in to find her six-year-old licking the kitten.

Trying to remain calm, she stopped her. "What are you doing?" she asked.

"I'm cleaning her like the momma cats do," her daughter said, spitting hair from her mouth. "I've done it four times since we got her. That's why she is so clean and pretty."

And that's when my sister had to explain that when she said for her little daughter to be like a mother to the kitten, she didn't mean *exactly* like a mother.

Election Time

It's almost primary election time. In our rural community, one of the most important local offices is the school board. It can be a thankless job. Anyone who has a child in school has definite opinions on how the school should be run and the most important uses of the money. And those with no children in school feel that bonds and levies are a waste of money, and the school board needs to cut spending and be more efficient.

In a previous election year, no one was running for the school board position in the district where I live. Everyone was encouraging someone else to do it. I even had people talk to me about it.

"You really ought to run," Old Evan said. "You're one of the most-looked-up-to people in the community. Everyone would vote for you."

"That's exactly why I don't plan to run," I replied.

"Why? Because you're one of the most-looked-up-to people in the community, and it might lower people's opinion of you?"

"No," I replied. "Because everyone might vote for me."

Eventually, my neighbor, Bart, decided to run. Bart is well-known, and everyone respects him. He does have strong opinions on issues, but he always tries to do what he feels is right.

He won unopposed, and that year, there were some major challenges for the school board. The state cut back funding, and the school board had to make decisions on where to cut expenses. The biggest possible budget that could be decreased was the sports programs. But parents of athletes are often the most outspoken, so that didn't go over well.

The programs for the arts was the second consideration. That includes music, art, and theatre. But more than 50% of the students are in those programs. The parents whose children were involved in the arts pointed out that the amount of money spent there was already the lowest when calculated on a per-child basis.

The school board proposed having a supplemental levy, but farm commodity prices were down, and since the levy would be a property tax, farmers came to the school board meeting in droves to complain. Those who had large summer cabins complained as well. Their children didn't go to school here, and they didn't feel they should pay increased taxes.

The school board worked hard to balance all the issues, but no one was happy. By the time the next election year rolled around, Bart had had enough. He told me he didn't plan to ever run again.

But no one else was running, and an incumbent would look like a quitter if he didn't run when he was unopposed. So Bart finally, reluctantly registered to run. And then, just before the filing deadline, Melanie registered, too, but she had less than a month to get the word out.

As I was driving home on the week of the election, I saw Bart out putting up signs along the roads. I laughed, thinking that his competitive spirit must have gotten the best of him. I waved and continued on my way. A few minutes later, he came around the neighborhood passing out campaign flyers.

"Don't forget to vote," he said.

I smiled as he left. Then I looked at the flier. It was a campaign ad for Melanie. Curiosity got the best of me, and I climbed into my car and drove to look at one of the signs Bart had been putting in along the road. Sure enough, it was for Melanie.

At a community gathering the day after the election, Bart was all smiles.

"Well, it was close, but we did it," he said.

"You won?" Evan asked.

Bart shook his head. "No. Melanie did by forty-two votes. Thank heaven."

I laughed. I had never seen someone so happy about losing.

A Mother Teaching Responsibility

Mother's Day was coming the next week, and the teacher for the men's group at church was leading a discussion relative to the importance of women in our lives.

"So, would any of you like to share a story about a woman who changed your life?" the teacher asked.

A few men shared a story or two. Then Bart, who everyone knew had been quite a prankster when he was young, raised his hand. The teacher called on him.

Bart smiled. "I guess I can share this story about my mother, even though I'm not sure what she would say if she knew I told you. But I can credit her for turning my life from one of constantly doing things that probably bordered on the edge of criminal to one that is better.

"The girls in the community always had a summer camp they all attended for a week. There would usually be over a hundred girls and their leaders, so the woman who was chosen to be the camp director had to be a no-nonsense kind of woman. She needed to be tough but loving. It happened that one year, the woman asked to take on this assignment was my mother."

Bart paused and looked at us and grinned. "You all know my mother, and you know that she is just that kind of woman. I knew it as well because I had pushed the boundaries with her many times.

"One of the things that the guys my age always did as a joke was to sneak into the girls' camp and play some pranks. We might do stuff like tip over an outhouse, or take girls' clothes drying on clotheslines and throw them into the pool. But if we were really daring, we would try to toilet paper the women leaders' cabin or do something else to it.

"Knowing it was my mother in charge, I almost didn't sneak into the camp with my friends, but they eventually talked me into it. We snuck in and had pulled a few pranks when one the boys suggested we should hit the leaders' cabin.

"I tried to talk them out of it, reminding them my mother was the one in charge, but they said that was all the more reason we should do it. I reluctantly agreed, and we moved a portable outhouse in front of the cabin door. I thought that would be a safe prank since the women couldn't get out to get us.

"But the women heard us and opened their door, only to find it blocked. We boys scattered, laughing, until we heard the air horn. Some men were stationed around the camp to watch for us, and the horn was a signal to them. The women couldn't get out of their cabin, but they could still blow the horn. The men converged on us, and soon, all five of us boys were rounded up. The men moved the outhouse to let the women out, and we boys quickly found ourselves standing in front of my mother.

"The sheriff was called, and when he and a deputy arrived, my mother pointed at the other four boys and said, 'You can do what you want with these four.' Then she pointed at me and said, 'But this one goes to jail for the rest of the week until girls' camp is over.'"

"Did they actually arrest you?" Old Evan asked.

Bart nodded. "That was a Tuesday, and my mom didn't come to get me out of jail until the next Monday."

"That's pretty harsh for a few pranks," Evan said.

"To be honest, I wasn't too concerned about spending a week in jail," Bart said. "What I was afraid of, and rightly so, was the punishment I would have when I faced my mom and dad."

"Was it pretty bad?" I asked.

Bart nodded. "I tried to blame it on my friends, but that just made it worse, since my mom said I needed to learn to not let my friends talk me into doing bad things. But the punishment helped me realize that even the smallest of deeds can have consequences."

Bart smiled. "And that's why I appreciate my mother."

A Friendly Community

There are many things that indicate the friendliness of a community, but the greatest is the desire of people to help their neighbors. I have experienced that helpfulness, and I saw it again in a humorous way this weekend.

Sunday was a beautiful sunny day, the first after a couple of weeks of rainy weather. At church, it was hard to contain the youth in the classes long enough to get through a lesson. Trying to take them outside to teach them while they enjoyed the sunshine didn't help. They basked in the warmth and didn't pay attention to anything that was being taught. When church ended, the youth burst out the doors into the fresh air, much like energetic young creatures coming out of hibernation.

The adults were affected by this spring fever, as well. Instead of visiting in the church foyer, as was usual, the conversations moved outside into the parking lot. I, too, went outside. As I was slowly moving to my car, I watched one family who was new to our community.

The wife, Brenda, said to her husband, "Honey, could you drive the children home? I think I would like to walk home today."

"Good luck with that," I said.

Brenda looked at me with surprise. "It's not that far," she said. "It can't be much more than a mile."

"It's not the distance," I replied. "It's the neighbors. Everyone is too friendly."

Brenda laughed. "How can neighbors be too friendly?"

"You'll see," I replied.

Brenda walked toward the road. Her husband and children passed her and waved on their way home. They were barely gone when Brenda settled into a nice casual stroll. But she hadn't walked more than fifteen yards when the first car stopped.

The driver rolled down his window. "Do you need a ride?" I heard him ask.

Brenda shook her head. "Just out for a pleasant walk home."

The friendly driver visited with her for a few minutes, and I could hear the angst in Brenda's voice as she must have desired to be on her way. Finally, the driver pulled out around Brenda and continued on his down the road.

Brenda hadn't gone another twenty yards when the next car stopped. Once more, the driver rolled down the car window, and I heard the familiar words. "Do you need a ride?"

I was barely within earshot, but I could sense the frustration in Brenda's voice as she said she was just enjoying the walk. The driver visited with her for a few minutes, then drove on.

As another car approached, Brenda appeared to quicken her pace. But she hadn't made it too far when the third car stopped. By this time, she was too far away for me to hear, but I could imagine that the conversation was much like the previous ones.

Instead of heading home, I decided to continue watching. Brenda's pace had changed from a pleasant walk to an almost-jog. But as I watched, three more cars stopped before she had even covered a hundred yards.

I climbed into my car and started on my way home. I watched ahead of me as cars continued to stop to offer Brenda a ride. When it was my turn, I pulled up alongside and rolled down my window, but I didn't stop. Instead, I kept pace with her.

"Now do you understand what I meant about the neighbors being too friendly?" I asked.

Brenda sighed. "I guess it's possible after all."

"That's why when I walk home, I cut through fields or follow the train tracks," I said.

With that, I continued on my way, but I smiled as I watched in my rearview mirror as the next car stopped to offer Brenda a ride.

Marie

We had just moved into the house where we now live when we met Marie. She was a sweet widow, a little grandmotherly lady whom our children soon referred to as "Grandma Moon." Marie was fiercely independent. Though she only had a small social security check to support herself, she was determined to pay her way through life.

She raised a nice garden and tried to supplement her income in any way she could. I did what I could to help her. Every spring, I ran my tiller down the street and tilled up her garden. My children excitedly came with me. The minute they saw me roll the tiller around to the front of the house, they knew where I was headed and hurried to join me. While I tilled, Marie sat in the chair she kept on her front porch, the children sat on the lawn, and Marie told them stories. Sometimes, when I stopped by with extra meat or milk, she would share her stories with me.

Our visits always ended the same way. As I prepared to leave, she would always ask, "So, how much do I owe you?"

I always answered the same, "Marie, the stories you share with my children are pay enough." Or I might say, "Milk was two for the price of one, so I couldn't just leave the extra gallon there when I knew you could use it."

The reason I gave for not accepting her money was usually not 100 percent factual, but I knew she couldn't afford meat or milk or other things like that. I hoped God would forgive my untruths, but I knew if she thought I purchased something extra for her, she would never accept it without paying me back. My good wife also prepared extra food for our meals and sent it with the children to Marie and had them tell her it was leftovers.

Marie always looked for ways to do something for us, so a person had to be careful. I made the mistake one day of telling her how beautiful her one lilac bush was. I love lilacs, and it was different from any I had ever seen. It had smaller, thicker pink flowers that gave it a smoky look. The problem was, the minute I mentioned it was pretty, Marie wanted me to have it.

"Oh, I couldn't take it, Marie," I said. "It's so beautiful right here, and I love to see it when I drive by your house."

Marie told me it was a special lilac, one that had been handed down through generations of her family. It wasn't very big, but she carefully tended it. I was only able to convince her to keep it by promising I would accept the first baby plant that grew from its roots.

Most lilacs put out a lot of starts, but this one rarely did. It was years before a start grew, and during that time, Marie always insisted, "You feel free to take some flowers if you want, whether I'm here or not." And she was happy the day she showed me a baby lilac under the bush that I could plant in my own yard. She told me that officially made me part of her family.

As the years went by, Marie grew older and feebler. Sometimes, my children would go to visit only to run home to get me because Marie had fallen or had something else happen. I would rush to her aid, and we would get her help. She would get better and would scold me, telling me she was ready to go join her husband, Les.

But one day when I ran to Marie's home and found her gasping for breath, I knew she wouldn't come home again. I made her as comfortable as I could until the ambulance arrived. The last thing she told me was that even after she was gone, I should stop and pick bouquets of lilacs.

Marie left us that day to join Les, and her home has since fallen into disrepair. But her little lilac has thrived and grown into a big bush. Its flowers open a little later than the other lilacs, and stay a little longer, so it's almost always still blooming on Memorial Day. That's the day I like to stop and pick a bouquet of flowers from it. I pick them to lovingly place on the grave of a sweet little lady who touched my life and the lives of my family.

What You Can Learn From Children

When I was asked to be the music teacher for all the children in our congregation who were under twelve years old, I was scared to death. I had never led music before. In our church, we call the organization that works with children of that age "primary." The woman who was the primary leader told me the most important thing was to just love the children.

That was the one thing I knew I could do. I loved the children, and after I learned to let go of my fear of making a fool of myself, it became the greatest assignment of my life. That is not to say that I didn't still make a fool of myself. I just learned that it didn't matter to the children when I did.

One spring, I decided we should sing a few songs for the season. We had just finished singing a song about baby animals being born and how life was new, when a little four-year-old boy raised his hand.

"Yes, Jeremy," I said. "What do you want?"

"Baby animals don't just get born in the springtime," he said.

"That's true," I replied. "Baby animals are born all year long."

"Did you know our dog had puppies last fall?" Jeremy asked.

"No, I didn't," I replied. "I'm sure that was a lot of fun."

"And I got to see baby chicks hatch this last winter," Jeremy added. "They were all fuzzy and cute and barely fit in the egg."

"Watching a baby chick being born is really amazing, isn't it?" I said.

"I asked my dad how the baby chick got into the egg," Jeremy said. "The eggs we eat don't have any baby chicks in them. My dad explained to me all about how animals get born and why the baby birds were in there."

I was sure that this was quickly turning into a lesson on the birds and the bees, and that was the last thing I wanted to talk about during music time for children, especially at church. I decided that I should try to change the subject.

"That's nice that you and your dad had a good talk about it," I said. "How about we sing another song about springtime?"

"But don't you want to know about how baby chicks get in the eggs?" Jeremy asked.

"Well, that is probably something that is special and should be shared just between you and your dad," I replied.

But Jeremy was not to be dissuaded. He wanted to impart his newfound knowledge.

"My dad said that when a person just has hens, there can't be any baby chicks," Jeremy said. "Did you know that?"

"Uh, yes, Jeremy," I replied, "I did know that."

"My dad said that a person has to have a rooster," Jeremy said.

"How about we sing a song about growing gardens and how God gives us sunshine and rain to make them grow?" I interjected.

But Jeremy didn't miss a beat. "That's why we don't have any eggs with chicks in them," he said, "because we don't have any roosters."

"That too bad," I replied. "Well, let's sing . . ."

"So, you see," Jeremy interrupted, "the eggs the hens lay don't have baby chicks in them, and that's why we eat those eggs. It's only the eggs that roosters lay that have the baby chicks. I think that after our hens get old and die, the next time we should get all roosters so we can have rooster eggs and have baby chicks."

I smiled. "I guess you'll have to take that up with your dad, Jeremy."

It truly is amazing the things a person can learn from children.

Pirates, Romans, and Scouts

It has been a few years since I've officially been a scoutmaster. Years ago, I had as many as eighteen boys in my troop. Even after I moved on to other assignments, I still spent a lot of time camping with the boys when their scoutmaster needed another adult.

But now I'm scoutmaster again. I hadn't been in long when a couple of the boys came to me and asked about going camping.

"When?" I asked.

"How about this weekend?" was their reply.

The weekend was only three days away, hardly time to do the planning.

"I have a pond with an island and canoes," I said. "Would you like to camp there? My scouts used to camp there off and on when we didn't have time to go anywhere else."

Some of the boys who hadn't been to my place thought that sounded "dumb." But the boys who had been fishing in my pond were excited and convinced the others it would fun.

Friday night arrived, and the boys showed up and set up their tents. They found that it was a nice place to camp. The island became our eating area with a fire pit and tables. The open area farthest from the road was for the tents. With the large number of trees, it was secluded and much like camping in the forest without the hours of travel.

After the camp was set up and the tents were pitched, which was my first rule of camping, the boys immediately went to the two canoes and the pedal boat. I began to wonder if my canoes would hold up under the imagination of the nine boys.

As I watched one canoe approaching the other at full speed, I heard one boy call out to the others in it, "Roman Army, ramming speed!"

The boys in the other canoe were able to turn just in time so they were only sideswiped. A boy in the second canoe yelled, "Avast, ye scurvy Roman dogs, prepare to be boarded by me band of pirates!"

The two groups of boys battled it out, taking prisoners and treasure. Treasure happened to be the paddles, and if one group could steal all the treasure from the other boat, leaving that boat stranded with no way to move, they would win. Sometimes the pirates won, and sometimes the Romans did, but most of the time, both canoes limped away in retreat from the fracas.

My old canoes already had some cracks, and the cracks were lending themselves to boat sinkings. So, after a few battles, the canoes were pulled onto shore for dry dock. They were patched with duct tape until they were more tape than boat, then they were relaunched to battle again.

After an hour or so of battling, I told the boys the Dutch oven potatoes were ready, and they needed to come cook hot dogs. The boys decided to skip the bridge and see how many they could fit onto the pedal boat. They started with one in each seat. That made four. Two more sat between them. With six, the poor boat was barely above the waterline.

One more boy, Jason, decided to stand on the back of the boat. Water trickled over the edge of the boat, and those in the back seats bailed water while the others pedaled.

Jason called out to me. "Hey, look, Daris, seven of us can fit on the pedal boat. Of course, if you were on it, you would be the only one, or it would sink. And it might sink anyway."

I laughed, but not because of what he said. He was facing backward as he yelled to me, and the boys were pedaling toward a low tree limb.

"Look at me," Jason said, striking a pose while still standing on the back facing me. "I'm George Washington crossing the Delaware."

Just then, the branch caught him across the shoulders, tumbling him into the water, and George Washington never made it across the Delaware that night.

As the boys gathered, shivering around the fire, I thought about how nice it was to be a scoutmaster again.

Singing to a Father

I was asked to teach music to the children at the church I attended. The children were from three to twelve, and we called it primary. I felt very inadequate, but the leader of primary told me the main thing I needed to do was to love the children.

And I did love the children. I loved them as if they were my own and thought of them that way. I was especially fond of one little girl. Millie loved to sing, but she sang monotone. She sang as loud as she could, and though she was only four, she almost matched all the other children put together. One day, as primary was ending, one of the teachers pulled me aside.

"Don't you think you should see if you can get Millie to sing quieter?" she asked.

"Why?"

"Well, she sings so, . . . so. . . " The teacher paused as if she was unable to say it.

"She sings so what?" I asked.

"She sings so badly," the teacher said.

"I don't think so," I replied. "I love to hear her little voice so full of enthusiasm."

"But next week is Fathers' Day, and you're having the children sing to their fathers. Don't you think her father will be embarrassed?"

"Not in the least," I replied. "If Millie were my child, I would be pleased to have her sing with such happiness."

The teacher just rolled her eyes and walked away.

I truly did not agree with her. I loved hearing Millie's monotone voice. It was a happy child's voice, and when she sang, it lifted my spirit, even if she wasn't on key.

But there was one child I was concerned about. David was eight, and something seemed to bother him. He sang quietly if he sang at all. Usually, he just stared at the floor. But when we sang a song he really liked, he would sing a little and seemed happier.

When we practiced the song for the fathers for the next week, I gathered the children around me. David stood outside the group, staring at the floor. I went and knelt in front of him.

"David, I would love to hear you sing. You have such a beautiful voice."

He looked at me with surprise showing in his face. "Do you really think so?"

"Yes, I do."

As we continued to practice, David's whole demeanor changed immediately. He looked up, smiled, and sang every song.

The next week, when the children gathered to sing for the fathers, David sang out, though with a little bit of timidity. When we went to primary, I had treats for the children and praised all of them, but I gave a little extra praise to David.

When church ended, David's mother came to me. She started to cry but finally was able to speak.

"I don't think you have any idea what you have done for David," she said. "David used to sing monotone, and a few years ago, when we attended another church congregation, the primary music teacher told him he had a terrible voice and asked him to be quiet. He quit singing altogether. Last week he told us he wouldn't sing for the fathers today, but after church last week, he happily said he had changed his mind. He told us what you said." She paused a moment, smiled, and said, "Thank you."

After she left, I pondered about what she said and considered what might have happened to Millie if the teacher had had her way. I thought that God surely loves to hear the smallest child happily sing, no matter how monotone or off-key the child is.

Millie's mother eventually signed Millie up with a singing

group, and over time, Millie blended better and sang on key. And though I loved to hear her sing with her new expertise, I admit that I missed her enthusiastic little four-year-old monotone voice.

And I'm sure her father did, too.

A Gringo

I looked at the menu, and I didn't understand a word on it. I hadn't been in Peru long, and I spoke almost no Spanish. I was traveling with a group from the university, and we were there not as tourists but to learn. During the first few days, the meals had been planned for us, but for this one, we were on our own. I had made my way downtown in Lima and found a restaurant that looked clean and appeared to have local cuisine. The picture of steaks on the front told me they probably served beef. That gave me the confidence that I could order okay.

I joined the line of people waiting to order. I listened intently to what each person was saying, but they spoke so fast, I didn't understand any of it other than a few numbers here and there. A year in advance of our trip, we each received books of key Spanish phrases along with tapes to listen to. I had studied them diligently. But the speaker on the tapes said everything clearly and slowly. What I heard now was a jumble of sounds to my ears.

When it was my turn to order, the menu looked like it was in a foreign language. Come to think of it, it was, but it was even more foreign than I expected. The teenage boy taking orders asked me what I wanted. At least that's what I assume he asked. I didn't have the slightest idea what to order. All the Spanish I learned just disappeared from my brain. The only word I could think of was "banyo" (bathroom). That one was drilled into us on the tapes in case we got into a desperate situation, but it didn't really apply at the moment.

At least I could read the prices. The numbers were the same as in the US. If I could do nothing else, I could consider the cost. Not knowing what else to do, I asked, "What would you recommend?"

The young man looked at me like I had just returned from an alien abduction. "No hablo Ingles."

I had learned the phrase, "No hablo Español" and knew it meant I didn't speak Spanish. What he said was close enough that I was sure he was telling me he didn't speak English.

I was holding up the line, and I could see that he was getting impatient with me. Finally, the young man called over his manager, and I moved aside so others could order.

The manager asked, "You order?"

I thought to myself, "Finally, someone who speaks English."

"Can you tell me what some of the things on the menu are?" I asked.

He shook his head. "No understand."

I realized he had just about used up most of the English he knew. I would just have to read off the menu the best I could. I decided that since I didn't know what anything was, I would just order something cheap. If I liked it, great. If not, I wasn't out a lot of money.

I looked at the cheap section of the menu, and I determined it must be similar to a value menu at fast-food restaurants in the United States. I decided to order from it.

"Salsa de tomate," I said, trying to sound as Spanish as possible.

I was sure the surprised look on his face was due to my good Spanish accent. I had listened to a lot of tapes.

That was only a small amount of money, so I thought I'd add more to it. I read something else from the cheap menu: "mostaza."

He nodded and smiled. I decided to add one more item. "Salsa de chile."

He grinned, took my money, and made change. It cost about the equivalent of a dollar. He left and was soon back with my order. He handed me a sack and a cup of water.

"Agua," he said. "With salsa de chile, you need."

I looked in the bag and found I had a small container of ketchup, one of mustard, and one that had a picture of five chili peppers on it. Apparently, I had ordered off of the condiments menu.

I must have looked embarrassed because the manager grinned.

"Next time," he said, "you go McDonald's and order chicken nuggets."

Cat Names

One of our cats had kittens this week. They are, I suppose, quite cute. Cats have never been my favorite animal, though there was one that I ended up liking. Its mother was killed by coyotes, so I raised it on a bottle. But usually, I view cats as annoying creatures that tend to trip me when I have an armful of something, or that tend to wrap themselves around my ankles as if I wanted them to.

Because of my lack of attachment to cats, I can never seem to remember what the other family members choose to name them. They use fancy names like Shimmer, Duchess, or Princess. I usually call them by how they look or act.

For example, we have a cat that was born perfectly white. I started out calling him Snowball. But then his coat changed, and he had an orange tinge within the white. It changed in the summer when we would eat popsicles. I started calling that cat Creamsicle.

Another cat was mostly black with a white belly. I called him penguin. Another one that looked like him I called Tux. One cat especially kept wrapping himself around my feet when I tried to walk. Once in a while, I would end up stepping on him, and he would let out a screech and run to hide. He would sulk for a few days then be right back to his idiotic pestering. I less-than-affectionately named him Dumb Dumb. Another cat had a tail that had a strange twitch to it. No matter what he was doing, his tail would flicker, even if he slept. That one got the name of Twitch. Other cats received the names Grey Kitty, Orange Kitty, and Black Kitty.

The thing about it, I could use the names I called them, and everyone knew exactly which cat I was talking about. But when the others in the family used the names they designated, such as Cuddles, Precious, Charlotte, or Zinnia, how was I to know which one that went with? Even the one I called Sylvester was obvious to anyone who had watched Saturday morning cartoons.

However, a problem with this naming convention of mine arose when it was me who started taking them to the vet. I remember the first one. The receptionist brought up our family account on the computer.

"What's the cat's name?" she asked.

I stood there trying to remember the name the kids had given it, but my mind was blank.

The receptionist looked up, somewhat impatiently. "This is your cat, right?"

"Yes," I replied. "But I can't think of the name my kids use."

"What do you call it?" she replied.

"Doormat," I replied.

"Doormat?" she said.

"Yes," I replied. "It always lies right in front of the door, so I step on it if I'm not looking."

"I suppose it doesn't matter what you call it as long as you know which cat it is," she said.

I was relieved. I thought she was going to give me a lecture about how cats are people, too, and should have proper names. I had received that lecture from my mother-in-law.

I continued taking the cats to the vet as needed, just registering them with the names I called them. But one day I came home, and my wife was holding a postcard.

"Perhaps I should be the one to take the cats to the vet from now on," she said.

"Why?" I asked.

"Because the mailman got a real good laugh out of this postcard."

I took the card and read it.

"Just a reminder that it's time for Hitler Cat's and Clown Kitty's shots."

Perhaps it would be better if someone else took the cats to the vet.

A Sense of Balance

Butch was always one to try to show everyone up. There was never an end to what he would brag that he could do. That's why what he claimed that day didn't surprise us.

"I watched a man walk a tightrope last night on TV," Butch said.

"Yeah. He was really good," Buster, Butch's brother, said.

"Well, I could walk a tightrope just as well if I wanted to," Butch said.

"Bet you couldn't," Buster replied.

"If we had one, I'd show you," Butch replied.

"Well, we don't have any rope like that," I said. "But maybe I can get a board and put it on its edge."

We were building on our barn, so we had lots of boards. I found one that was two inches thick, ten inches wide, and about twenty feet long. We stood it on its edge, and Buster held one end, and I held the other. Butch stepped up on it. He had only taken one step when he fell off.

"I knew you couldn't do it," Buster said.

"That's because there's no real motivation to stay on," Butch said. "This is no challenge. The guy on TV last night walked high above the ground. He had the motivation to stay on to not get hurt."

"That's true," Buster said. "If you fall off, you'll only fall ten inches. Big deal."

"If we tried to set it up high off the ground, my dad would kill me," I said.

"I know," Buster replied, "let's set it up over the manure pit. That would give Butch motivation to not fall off."

Butch agreed that it would be motivation, and I felt it wouldn't be too dangerous. So Buster walked his end around the manure pit. Buster and I set the board up, and Butch was just about ready to step onto it when Buster stopped him.

"Wait a minute," Buster said. "The guy on TV last night was carrying a girl on his shoulders. If you feel you can do as well, you should carry something."

We looked around and couldn't think of anything, and then Butch spied the piglets. They were about twenty pounds each.

"How about I carry a piglet?" Butch asked.

"They don't weigh near as much as a girl," Buster said.

"How about two piglets?" Butch replied.

We all agreed that would be a reasonable feat. So, we caught two piglets. They were squealing and squirming as Butch tucked one under each arm. He was now ready for the challenge.

With Buster and me holding the ends of the board tight against the ground above the manure pit, Butch stepped out onto it. He wobbled, but regained his balance and took a step. He wobbled a bit more than the first time but regained his balance. As he started to take the next step, one piglet started to squeal and wiggle harder. This upset the other one, and it did the same. Butch tried to take a step, but with the wiggling piglets, he was wobbling so much he knew he wouldn't make it.

Realizing he was in trouble, he must have decided he could run across the board. He took a few quick steps, but this just took him to the deepest part of the pit. He was wobbling a little more on each step, and then he missed the board altogether. But he was leaning so far forward trying to run, that he didn't drop straight down into the manure that would have come to about his waist. Instead, he face-planted with one piglet still under each arm.

The squealing piglets wriggled free and swam to the edge. Butch came up sputtering.

Buster called out. "Hey Butch, I bet you're glad we put the board over the manure pit so you had a soft landing and weren't hurt."

I think I would have rather been hurt.

A Fourth of July Surprise

For me, the Fourth-of-July celebration started early. The scouts in our community put flags up in front of every house on holidays. In return, many of the people in our community donated to our scout program. Even if a person couldn't afford to donate, they would still find a beautiful flag waving in the breeze outside their house when they woke up. As a scoutmaster, I was up by five-thirty helping the boys get the flags in place.

When I arrived back home at six-thirty, I found my daughter Elliana preparing to go to work at McDonald's. She had to start at seven-thirty in the morning and work until late afternoon. That meant she couldn't even go to the flag-raising or the community breakfast. She also would miss the parade and most other celebratory events.

I would usually be the one who would take Elli to work, but this morning, I knew I needed to be with my scouts at the flag-raising. As I left, my wife headed to town with Elli.

The flag-raising and breakfast went well. The speaker did a good job and had some wonderful patriotic music and a slide show. We had all sorts of muffins, juice, and milk. Mostly, it was just a fun time to visit. But I didn't enjoy it as much as I might have. All I could think of was Elli having to work and missing it.

It wasn't long after the breakfast was over before we were heading to the parade. We went to my mother's house and picked her up, and by ten o'clock, we were setting up chairs on the parade route. Another daughter and her husband also met us there.

The Ashton parade is everything a small community parade should be: lots of horses, tractors, antique automobiles, and old farm equipment. But then came my favorite part. After the parade had all gone by, everyone went into the street and visited. Then, after a little while, the parade came back, going the other way, and everyone moved to the side.

My father used to say, "A parade is only as good as the number of friends you meet."

This community parade is the best there is in that way.

After the parade, we went to a small café and ate lunch. The food was good, and we had a fun time just visiting with each other and with people who came in. After we could hardly eat another bite, we had some of the best ice cream served anywhere. The whole time, however, all I could think of was buying extra pizza and ice cream for Elli to enjoy later.

After we took Mom home so she could get a well-deserved nap, it was finally time to pick Elli up from work.

When she came out and climbed in the car, I said, "I wish you could have been with us and not had to miss everything."

She smiled. "I felt bad missing it, too. But I had my own simple but wonderful Fourth-of-July surprise."

"What was that?" I asked.

"I was working the drive-thru," she said. "A man pulled up and paid for his food. Then he said he wanted to pay for everyone in the vehicle behind him. I looked at the bill for the vehicle behind him, and it was a fair amount. I asked the man if he was sure he wanted to pay for it. He assured me he did.

"I told him that was really nice and asked him if he knew them. He shrugged and said, 'Sort of. In a way, we all do.' I asked him if he wanted me to tell them anything. He smiled and said, 'Just tell them thank you.'

"And when the next vehicle pulled up, guess who was in it?"

"Who?" I asked.

"It was a big van full of soldiers and veterans. When I told them the man ahead of them had paid the bill and told them what he said, I felt like I would cry."

She finished by saying, "I may have missed the celebration, but I had the best Fourth-of-July surprise ever."

The Dowry

I joined some other men and women to take the youth of our community to a waterslide for the evening. I went down the slide only once and felt my body would never be the same. Most of the other adults felt the same way about the slide, so while the youth continued to see who could go the fastest or fly the farthest without killing themselves, we adults visited and grew fat eating brownies.

Our community is rural, and talk among the men soon turned to crops and cattle. From there, it turned to milk cows and how much time they took. At one point, Doug, one of the men there, turned to me.

"Daris, didn't you grow up on a dairy farm?" he asked.

"I sure did," I replied. "And I had milk cows until recently. How about you?"

"I had one once," Doug replied. "It actually came in quite useful."

He then told me the story. He said that on the Saturday he got off of his honeymoon, his father-in-law showed up. He was driving a truck with a single cow in the back.

"This cow is yours, Doug," the father-in-law said. "I'm giving her to you as a dowry for my daughter."

Doug thought that was a down-right gentlemanly thing to do. He graciously accepted the cow. But Doug began to wonder when he saw the grin on his father-in-law's face.

Doug locked the cow in the old barn and fed her. That evening, he milked her. She was gentle, and there seemed to be no problem, so Doug just passed off his father-in-law's grin as friendliness.

The next morning, Doug had an early morning meeting at the

church. He decided to go to it, and then come home to milk. When he returned from the meeting, he was in for a surprise. The cow had busted her way out of the barn, and that is not figuratively. She truly busted down part of a wall.

Doug drove up and down the road, and finally found the cow about a mile away, mowing his neighbor's yard. The neighbor was not too keen on the free mowing job, and even less so about the free fertilizer the cow left on his doorstep.

Doug finally got a rope on the cow, and the minute he did, she took off down the road at full speed with Doug in tow. It was embarrassing enough to be flying down the road like a kite, but the cow had to make sure she looped through everyone's yard so they all would see Doug as human ballast on the end of the rope. The cow dragged Doug right past his house and finally came to a stop in a deep ditch. She then turned to sneer at him, and Doug was sure she was asking him what he planned to do about it.

Doug finally got the cow home and milked her. He was late for church, and he found his predicament and morning run was the talk of the community.

That night when Doug went out to milk the cow, all was well. But the next morning, he found she had busted another hole in the barn wall and was gone again. Doug was so mad he could hardly speak. He was sure his father-in-law had given him the cow because he knew she would do this. He went in to ask his wife.

"The stupid cow is out again," Doug said.

"Oh, you mean Lucy?" she replied. "You know she got her name because she was always on the loose-ee."

Doug's wife laughed, but Doug didn't think it was funny.

"But I did find a good use for the cow," Doug said to me.

"What was that?" I asked.

"The next day was the auction, and I found out that a cow sold for just enough money to buy a newly married couple a nice television," Doug said. "And that was the only useful purpose I have ever found for a milk cow."

What's Your Sign?

My daughter Celese was working at a fast-food restaurant. As employees often do, they would play jokes on each other.

Celese had worked there for a long time and had risen to the rank of manager. One day, it was her turn to manage the evening shift. As her shift was starting, the manager of the previous shift paused to give Celese some notes.

"The sign was changed earlier today," that manager told her.

That was always important to know. When a new special was put up on the sign, there was usually about a fifty-percent increase in sales of that item for a few days. The crews had to work harder to keep up with orders, especially on the foods that were discounted.

Celese went to look at the sign so she would know what her crew needed to keep ready. The sign said, "Check out our new hot chicken sandwiches. Try them today."

As Celese took over for her shift, she warned her crew to keep the chicken sandwiches cooking so they could keep up. For the first hour or so on her shift, it was all that her crew could do to keep the chicken cooked for the sandwiches. But after about an hour, something changed.

The number of people coming in increased dramatically, and sales were soaring. But it wasn't all chicken sandwiches. Those coming through were ordering many varieties of food. But there was another change, too. The customers were almost all boys, and they were making strange comments. They would say things like, "I love your sign," "I love your hot chicks," or "Hey, baby, what's your sign?"

The sales were through the roof, and her crew was exhausted from the constant rush of orders. But the strange things people were saying, and the fact that it was mostly boys ordering, made Celese wonder if something more than a new special was going on. And it all seemed to have something to do with the sign.

Finally, Celese went out to look at the sign, and to her dismay, she found it had been changed. Instead of what it had said, it read, "Check out our hot new chicks. See them today."

Celese realized that her crew was all girls, and she knew that the boys who worked at the restaurant must have changed the sign. She was annoyed and determined to change it back. She called the head store manager and told him there was a problem with the sign and asked him where a ladder was. He told her where it was, and she immediately went and pulled it out of the storage shed.

She found that the removed letters were sitting at the bottom of the sign. She had just set the ladder up and was climbing it with letters in hand when the restaurant owner showed up.

He looked at what the sign said, looked at Celese holding the letters, and said, "What do you think you're doing?"

Celese tried to explain that she was sure the boys must have changed the sign, and she was just trying to change it back. The store owner seemed less than believing and looked at her skeptically.

The next day, when the owner did the financial audit of the previous day, he seemed even more skeptical. There were bonus points given to crews who had high sales, and Celese's crew had higher sales than any shift had had for months.

"I appreciate you attempting to push up sales," he said to Celese, "but there are certain techniques that probably shouldn't be used."

Celese tried again to convince him that she hadn't done it, but she never was sure he ever believed her.

When Work Gets Tense

It was graduation week at the university in our small town. Students were finishing up finals and didn't have time to make their own food. Parents were coming into town and wanted to take their college children out for dinner. Because of this, the workers at the fast-food restaurants had to work extra hours. And they were exhaustingly busy hours, too. All this created a tense atmosphere at some of the restaurants, especially those with defined limits on how long it was supposed to be from the time food was ordered to the time it was delivered.

John, a friend of mine, was working at a hamburger place that had such a defined limit. The goal was ninety seconds from order to delivery. Though they didn't usually make that time, everything was compared to it. Making matters more intense, managers' evaluations were based on the average delivery time. As huge groups came in and the time for delivery went up, the shift managers often grew tenser.

But worse than taking a long time was getting an order wrong. It was especially bad when something was left out that had been paid for. When this happened, the item was not only provided, but a coupon for a free meal was given. This decreased profits and, in turn, became a negative mark for the manager of that shift.

John said that on one particular evening, the line to order food was often out the door. Customers were getting irate, adding to the problem. In addition, a couple of workers had called in sick, leaving the crew short-handed. Every employee there was working as fast as possible, and mistakes were inevitable.

A few customers ended up having items missing in their orders, and coupons had to be given. All this was making the manager tense; he was becoming terser with the other employees, and his voice was rising. John was one of those loading food onto trays or into sacks, and he caught his share of the manager's ire. It was right at that point that the unimaginable happened.

A man in a dark business suit, with a lady in a nice evening gown, stepped up to order. From John's vantage point, he could see those preparing the food, but he was also out near the front counter. As the man ordered, John saw one of the workers reach for the tartar sauce gun. The sauce guns looked like big caulk guns. A worker would pull the trigger just enough to give the right amount of sauce.

But the worker didn't get a good grasp on the tartar sauce gun, and it slipped from his grasp. It fell in the worst possible way, with the backside down. The mechanism with the spring that pushed the tartar sauce to the nozzle smashed against the cement floor. When this happened, it almost always shot the sauce onto the ceiling. All those preparing the food immediately looked up.

But John had seen the white stream of sauce pass right by him. He turned to the counter, and to his dismay, he saw it had made a big splotch on the customer's suit jacket. The face of the woman next to the man ordering went white, and instantly, everyone in the restaurant, employees and customers alike, went silent.

John said the manager just froze and didn't seem to know what to do. But the cashier was a young man named Seth who was known for his quick wit and humor. He looked at the big white splotch on the man's black suit and said, "Would you like a chicken sandwich with that?"

The man suddenly broke into laughter, and after a moment, the lady with him joined in. Soon, everyone was laughing: the customers in the foyer, the employees, and even the manager. The man and woman received their meals free and were given a washcloth and a coupon for the restaurant to pay for the dry cleaning of the suit. But the main thing that happened was that the tension was eased, and the whole atmosphere in the restaurant changed.

Humor has a way of doing that.

Community Teamwork

Too often it seems like all the news we hear is bad; at least a high percentage of it is negative. That's why I always look for positive, uplifting stories. There was an event that occurred over the last few weeks in our community that is worth retelling.

During this time of year in the West, we are often faced with dry conditions leading to major wildfires. This year, here in Idaho, we had an extremely wet spring. That is great for getting the crops off to a good start. But toward the middle to the end of June, the weather turned hot and dry. We hadn't had a good rain for a month or more.

The problem with this set of events is that the heavy spring rains also made the grass and shrubbery proliferate. But then when the rains quit and the sun heated everything, the grass and shrubs dried and became tinder for a fire. It made for a dangerous situation. Add to that dry lightning storms, with lightning strikes and no rain to quell the sparks, and the fire season turned explosive.

The dry rangeland to the north of us, thousands of acres of sagebrush and prairie grass, was in this exact situation. Fires started, presumably from some dry lightning strikes. Soon, the fire was burning at high speed across the range. The fire crews rushed to save a small town that was in the fire's path. They didn't have resources to try to save the cattle that grazed this land.

This is where the wonderful part of the story comes together. The ranchers, farmers, and anyone else who could rushed to help those in need. People who work the land are often independent and determined to take care of their own needs, but what nature was throwing at them was more than anyone could face on their own.

Everyone involved came together and made a plan. It was determined what land would be most defensible. All cattle would be driven there and fenced in together. The concern of separating whose animals were whose would have to be dealt with later. While horse riders set out to bring in all the cattle that could be found, farmers took tractors and disks and harrowed the perimeter of the area where the cattle would be detained, determined to make a stand against the fire. By the time the cattle were rounded up and brought to the protected pastures, a large amount of soil had been turned to cover anything that would burn.

The fire came and burned through, sweeping everything in its path, but it could not cross the harrowed fields. The smoke was heavy and caused the sun to glow red if it showed at all. Farmers with tractors also helped the firefighters, harrowing to create fire breaks around towns and homes in the path of the fire. For a week it was hard to breathe as the fire burned, but when it was finally brought under control, the damage was minimal compared to what it could have been.

This valley is known for the early settlers coming into an arid, inhospitable land and working together to dig canals that would bring the life-saving water to the crops. To survive, neighbor helped neighbor. No single man could do it alone. And when the work was finished, everyone benefitted as the water flowed to all.

The people of this valley showed themselves to be worthy descendants of those early settlers. Even those whose land and homes were in well-irrigated areas and were not threatened by the fire worked as if their own land and subsistence were at stake. Everyone who was not needed on the front lines worked as support. It was a wonderful story of community teamwork.

When all is said and done, there are few stories more worth retelling than one of community teamwork.

Where Do Babies Come From?

I knew things were going to be interesting in my class of five-year-olds at church when Brittany came in. She looked like a walking storm cloud.

"Is something wrong, Brittany?" I asked.

She let out an elongated gasp. "Do I look like a baby to you?" she asked.

"No," I replied. "Why do you ask?"

"Because my family calls me 'the baby,' and I'm sick of it."

"Well, you are the youngest in the family," I said.

"And that's why I want a baby brother," Brittany said. "I've talked to my mother about it a thousand times, but she won't listen."

I had played Santa for our community the Christmas before. Brittany had asked me for a baby brother then, and Brittany's mother had scolded her for it.

"Have you told your family you don't like it?" I asked.

She nodded. "Mom and Dad try hard to remember not to say it, but my brother says it even more just to make me mad. If I don't get a baby brother, I'm about ready to run away from home."

Kaylee raised her hand, so I called on her.

"Where do babies come from, anyway?" she asked.

That's not a topic I wanted to address, so I said, "Maybe you should ask your parents."

"Daddy, don't you know?" my little daughter asked.

That felt like a strange question coming from my own child, and I didn't know what to say.

"I know, I know," David said excitedly. "I saw a movie where a stork brought the baby."

"That's stupid," Brittany said. "A stork isn't big enough to carry a baby."

"My daddy told me that you find a wishing star and wish on it," Leanna said. "Then you have to be patient for nine months until the baby is delivered to the hospital so you can pick it up."

"Kind of like slow shipping on Amazon, huh?" I asked.

Leanna nodded. "Really slow shipping."

"I saw a baby horse born," Tyler said. "It came right out of its momma, and it was yucky. I asked my dad how it got in there, and he said the momma horse must have swallowed a baby horse seed."

Brittany snorted with disgust. "Your dad must not know, either. There are no such things as horse seeds, and there definitely aren't any baby-brother seeds."

I decided it was time to get back to the lesson, but no matter how I tried, everything came back to how a baby is born. David mentioned that he saw a chicken come out of an egg. Susan said her cat had nine kittens all at once.

"Why don't people have nine babies all at once?" Susan asked.

"Because the parents would like a little sleep," I replied.

They didn't realize I was joking, and they continued on about babies while I kept trying to steer the discussion back to the lesson. But one little girl, Maelynn, never said a word. She was very smart and pondered ideas more than the rest. By the look in her eyes, I could see she was deep in thought. Finally, she raised her hand.

"I know where babies come from," Maelynn said.

As smart as she was, I was afraid she just might, but I couldn't stop the train now. Everyone turned to look at Maelynn, knowing that what she said was usually the right answer.

"My daddy told me that when two people really love each other, they adopt a baby so they can share even more love together. That's where I came from."

It was then that I remembered Maelynn was adopted.

The rest of the children accepted that as the absolute truth, and I smiled as they all settled down for the lesson, which just happened to be about the importance of families.

If you enjoyed this book, please leave a review on Amazon at:

Would you like to see the *Life's Outtakes* column running in your local paper or magazine? Suggest it to the editor. If an editor runs the *Life's Outtakes* column due to your suggestion, we will send you a free autographed book by Daris Howard. Find out more at:

http://www.darishoward.com

Read stories, purchase books, or subscribe to our short story list by going to:

http://www.publishinginspiration.com

Daris Howard's Amazon page:

https://www.amazon.com/dp/1629860220

For inspiring plays and books, as well as discounts for booksellers, go to

http://www.publishinginspiration.com

About the Author

Daris Howard, an award-winning author and playwright, grew up on an Idaho farm. He was a state champion athlete, competed in college athletics, and lived for a time in New York.

Daris has worked as a cowboy, a mechanic, in farming, and in the timber industry. He is now a college professor.

He has also been a scoutmaster, having up to eighteen boys in his scout troop at a time. In his wide range of experience, he has associated with many colorful characters who form a basis for his writing. Daris has had plays translated into German and French, and his plays have been performed in many countries around the world. For many years, Daris has written the popular column *Life's Outtakes*, which consists of weekly short stories and is published in various newspapers and magazines in the US and Canada.